BBC
DOCTOR WHO

A BRIEF
HISTORY OF

TIME
LORDS

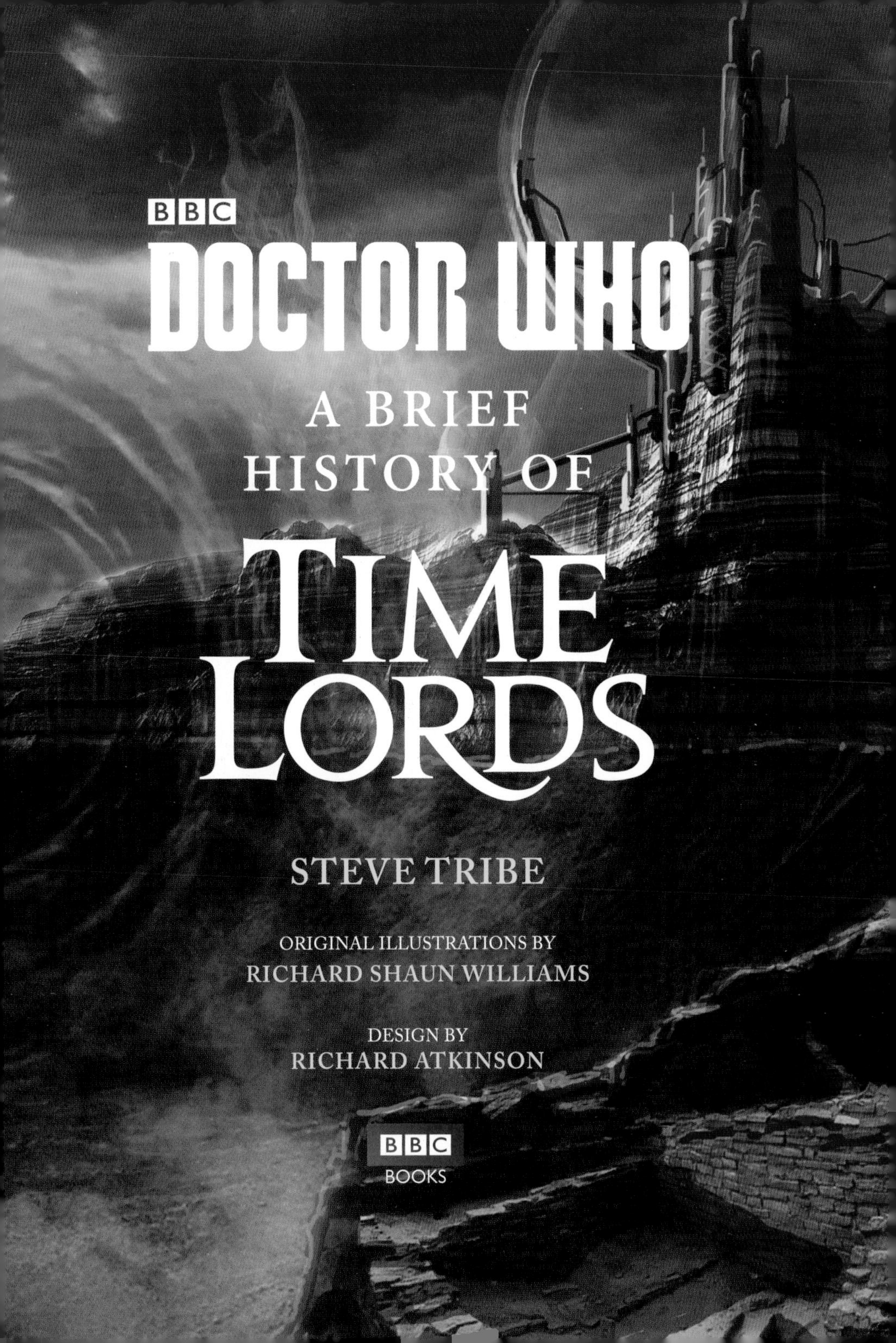

BBC

DOCTOR WHO

A BRIEF HISTORY OF

TIME LORDS

STEVE TRIBE

ORIGINAL ILLUSTRATIONS BY
RICHARD SHAUN WILLIAMS

DESIGN BY
RICHARD ATKINSON

BBC
BOOKS

1 3 5 7 9 10 8 6 4 2

BBC Books, an imprint of Ebury Publishing
20 Vauxhall Bridge Road,
London SW1V 2SA

BBC Books is part of the Penguin Random House group of companies
whose addresses can be found at global.penguinrandomhouse.com

Penguin
Random House
UK

This book is published to accompany the television series entitled *Doctor Who*
broadcast on BBC One. *Doctor Who* is a BBC Wales production.
Executive producers: Steven Moffat and Brian Minchin

First published by BBC Books in 2017

www.penguin.co.uk

A CIP catalogue record for this book is available from the British Library

ISBN 978 1 785 94216 7

Printed and bound in China by Toppan Leefung

Penguin Random House is committed to a sustainable future for our business, our readers
and our planet. This book is made from Forest Stewardship Council® certified paper.

GALLIFREY LIES in the constellation of Kasterborous, within a parsec or two of the centre of the galaxy, its binary location from Galactic Zero Centre being 10-0-11-00 : 02. The planet, its moons and its major settlements are shielded by a transduction barrier, and nothing can get past it.

Well, that's not true for a start.

GALLIFREY LIES in the constellation of Kasterborous, within a parsec or two of the centre of the galaxy, its binary location from Galactic Zero Centre being 10-0-11-00 : 02. The planet, its moons and its major settlements are shielded by hundreds of Sky Trenches, and nothing can get past them.

And that's not true either.

GALLIFREY LIES time-locked at the moment of its destruction on the final day of the Last Great Time War. It's dead. It burned. It's just rocks and dust.

And neither is any of that.

GALLIFREY LIES in the Sol system of Mutter's Spiral at galactic coordinates 58-0-44-68-48-84, occupying a portion of space formerly reserved for a planet called Earth.

Or perhaps that didn't quite come off.

GALLIFREY LIES frozen in a parallel pocket universe, having been saved from annihilation by the combined forces of thirteen Doctors.

Or it did, at some point. Probably.

GALLIFREY LIES in the constellation of Kasterborous, within a parsec or two of the centre of the galaxy, its binary location from galactic zero centre being 10-0-11-00 : 02. It is hidden at the extreme end of the time continuum, for its own protection. We're at the end of the universe, give or take a star system.

Hmm… Maybe there is only one thing we can say with any degree of certainty:

GALLIFREY LIES.

THEY THAT WALK IN THE SHADOWS

Some would say that's unfair, that it's the Time Lords who lie. Don't blame Gallifrey; blame Rassilon. Out there in the cosmos, a belief that history is written by the victors is widely understood to be the mark of a Level Five civilisation. We Time Lords, of course, transcended such simplistic concepts when the universe was less than one-fifth of its present size. History, we understand, is rewritten by its future.

Or possibly – as I found once that I will have written in the Preface to the Seventh Edition – history is hogwash.

The official hogwash is almost entirely fabricated, and only the myths and legends are true (partially, at least). No wonder the great and good of Gallifrey – the High Council, the Inner Council, the Cardinals of the Academy, the old men in the funny hats – are all so determined that you should never read this book.

The pages are slightly time-sensitive: anything I recall writing probably isn't here; what is here, I have already forgotten ever having been about to write it tomorrow. But if you're holding it now, in your hands, absorbing the words, learning and unlearning the heresies, then you know that this, at least, is one truth.

THE SHINING WORLD OF THE SEVEN SYSTEMS

There's an awful lot of planet out there. The Time Lords out-sit eternity inside a couple of protective bubbles, quivering at the mention of *outside*, never really seeing what's under our noses: Gallifrey is huge, and hugely beautiful.

What do we see, when we peer out of our little glass domes? Barren Drylands, bleak and cold. Ancient, twisted trees. Weeds sprouting among the bare grey rocks. Pathetic little patches of sludgy snow covering those ranges of forbidding, inhospitable mountains.

The Drylands

The Capitol – the glorious citadel enclosed in its mighty glass dome

Yet our world is simply glowing with life. The colours are deeper and richer than you could possibly imagine. The rocks aren't grey at all; they're red, brown, purple and gold. And those pathetic little patches of sludgy snow are shining white in the light of the twin suns. At night the sky is a burned orange, and the leaves on the ulanda trees are bright silver. When those leaves catch the light each morning, it looks like a forest on fire. When autumn comes, the breeze blows through the branches like a song.

At some point in our ancient and forgotten history, before we disinfected our lives, we Time Lords must have gazed at our home world and marvelled. When we looked out across the continent of Wild Endeavour and first saw the mountains, we didn't label them, we *named* them: Perdition, Serenity, Solace and Solitude… They go on and on for ever. Slopes of deep red grass, capped with snow. When the second sun rises in the south, those mountains shine.

There is so much life among those rolling red pastures, and so much colour: the small yellow Sarlains, the velvet-red *Madevinia aridosa*, the golden-green Schlenk blossom; the flies and flubbles and flutterwings, the cats and mice and rovies, the rabbits and tafelshrews, the pig-rats and plungbolls, the trunkikes and the yaddlefish… Officially, Gallifrey possesses the only eco-system in the universe not to have been ravaged and wrecked by its primary indigenous species – no animal has ever become extinct. Unofficially, of course, the Gallifreyans fought a war that ultimately destroyed the lot. Apart from the flies.

Or, rather, the *Time Lords* fought a war. Outside the citadels are the dismissed and the discarded of Gallifrey. Who has ever lived out there, in that barbarian garden? Outsiders, outcasts, rejects; a few mad souls who spurned the society of Time Lords. Shobogans. Nobody that matters. Except even *that* is not true: almost the whole population lives outside the cities. Billions of native Gallifreyans in their farms and homesteads, working through the day to feed themselves – and us – until the night-time comes…

Do you remember being just 7 years old? Those endless, restless nights, terrified of sleep because of the nightmares? And, if you're honest with yourself, what were those dreams about? Toclafane? Shakri? Snow White and the Seven Keys to Doomsday? No – the thing that every 7-year-old on Gallifrey truly dreads is turning 8. Being taken from their family and failing the

selection. What will *you* fail to become, child? Soldier? Chancellery Guard? Time Lord?

Or, worse, will you *pass*, and spend all your lifetimes inside one of those bubbles? Forget your past life, until it comes naturally to you to recoil from the outside, shut it out, condemn it. Perhaps you'll only cope with your sterile existence by shutting out all that life. Or by shutting yourself in.

THE CITADELS

The Capitol and Arcadia, Gallifrey's first and second cities – two great metropolises of towers stretching up into the heavens, anchored by vast wheels whose supports and vaults reach deep into the bowels of the planet.

Let's begin at the heart of the Capitol, indeed the heart of Gallifrey. Sector 1's main tower holds the Panopticon. Every great event of state is held within this vast hexagonal chamber. (It is believed that each of its six sides honours a founding father of Gallifrey, but since nobody can agree who they all were, the point is moot.) It has seen presidential inaugurations and presidential resignations, and even presidential assassinations. It's large enough to hold many hundreds of Time Lords, and designed in such a way that every point in the chamber is visible from every other point. Its walls reach higher than the naked eye can see, with a series of viewing galleries circling at every level.

The Panopticon

The Capitol Museum

To either side of the main entrance, discreet doorways lead to a series of antechambers where Time Lords gather to don their robes of state – the scarlet and orange of the Prydonians, the green of the Arcalians, the heliotrope of the Patrexes, and so on. A ramp leads from one of these antechambers directly onto the main dais, from which the President addresses his people.

Elsewhere in the tower is the Capitol Museum. Here can be seen the symbols of presidential office – the Crown, the Sash, the Rod – removed only on great occasions of state. The

Museum also displays examples of every kind of robe of state, from the President and the Gold Usher to the Chapter Cardinals.

With ceremonial duties largely carried out in and around the Panopticon, the Capitol's political heart is found in Sector 2. Here are the Council chambers – conference rooms for the Inner Council and other small gatherings, and an enormous assembly room for meetings of the full High Council.

The President's office lies adjacent to the Inner Council conference room. This

The presidential dais

The Inner Council conference room

The full High Council in session

office contains at least two hidden exits. The first leads to a hidden compartment, a secret room containing the controls for the forbidden Time Scoop (see Chapter 1). The second – another concealed passage – leads from Sector 2 directly to the Chancellor's office in the third sector.

Sector 3 is entirely given over to the Chancellor and the Chancellery Guard. The neighbouring Sector 4 holds the Castellan's office, the courtrooms and the Security Compound. The

The President's office

The Castellan's office

An interrogation cell

Space Traffic Control

Temporal Control

Compound itself comprises detention rooms, interrogation cells, and a selection of execution rooms, most of which are officially closed and disused by High Council decree.

The Capitol's hundreds of libraries, records rooms and archive stores constitute the fifth sector, with direct access to Sector 6, which houses the various Chapters of the Academy. After the Panopticon, this is the largest structure in the citadel, where every novice Time Lord is instructed. It also, for reasons best known to Rassilon, holds the main force-field control area for the transduction barrier that shields Gallifrey.

Sector 7 is dominated by the Communications Tower, site of both Space Traffic Control and Temporal Control, two of the highest security-rated rooms in the citadel. From here, the Time Lords monitor and log every passing vessel in Gallifrey's vicinity. It is believed that the same tower contains Gallifrey High Command's War Room, together with an extraction chamber for removing other beings from their time streams. Since Gallifrey High Command's War Room is subject to an even higher security rating and the existence of extraction chambers is officially denied, however, it's impossible to be sure.

The final area, Sector 8, is home to the Time Travel Capsule landing bays and an array of TARDIS repair shops. TARDISes that have reached the end of their lifespans are despatched to an area below the repair shops that's

Gallifrey High Command

Time Travel Capsule landing bay

A TT Capsule repair shop

The Panopticon Vaults

The Time Vaults

come to be known as the TARDIS Graveyards.

Somewhere in all of that lies a set of chambers allocated to the Celestial Intervention Agency (see Chapter 2). Nobody outside the Agency is certain where these might be. The conspiracy theorists claim that the CIA uses architectural configuration to destabilise the pedestrian infrastructure of the Capitol to constantly vary their temporospatial location within the citadel. But we don't want to listen to conspiracy theories, do we?

And somewhere *below* all that lie layer after layer of buried secrets. Deep beneath the Panopticon in the Panopticon Vaults is the Eye of Harmony (see Chapter 1). A warren of ducts and serviceways reveals a myriad mysterious and concealed adyta, scenes of countless plots and treasons. Deeper

still are the Cloisters, the dark and damp and misty physical location of the Matrix, guarded by the Cloister Wraiths.

And finally, buried as if in shame near the very core of the planet are the Time Vaults, home of the Omega Arsenal, where all the forbidden weapons are locked away.

Step back a moment, wherever you are at this moment, and look around you. Glass and metal, metal and glass, whichever way you look. Look down, look up. More glass, more metal, as far as you can see – you can't even see the sky. All around you are towers, too tall for you to even comprehend. The Communications Tower alone is some 53 storeys high, and you just can't take it in.

So… if *we* can't see these mighty edifices, just who are they meant to impress?

CHAPTER ONE

THE DARK TIMES

We Time Lords are an odd lot. Sitting for millennia, observing and recording the minutiae of every instant of every life form everywhere throughout existence – and yet our knowledge of our own history is so fragmentary. We know little, and admit to less.

When precisely, for instance, did we develop the capacity to regenerate? The Time Lord miracle: a complete physical and mental renewal, gifting ourselves new lives whenever we wish to, or when age, illness or accident forces us to. Did we emerge from the primordial soup with thirteen lives? Or did Rassilon sit in

The Sisterhood of Karn

his tower, playing with test tubes and genetic looms until he had woven just the right cocktail? And why *thirteen* lives? Is that an inherent natural restriction? We've long (always?) been able to dole out complete new regeneration cycles, so perhaps that magic 'thirteen' is some artificial limitation to prevent anyone going on just that little bit too long?

Maybe a clue lies on the planet Karn. It is accepted / suspected / rumoured (delete according to taste) that the Sisterhood of Karn originated on Gallifrey and is tied to the Time Lords until the End of Time. Since what we know as the Dark Time and what they call the Time of the Stones (which is

pithier?), the Sisterhood has shared the Elixir of Life with the Time Lords. The two races are equals in mental power, though the Sisterhood's telepathic and telekinetic abilities far outclass the Time Lords'. There are even some forbidden accounts that place the Sisterhood at the apex of the earliest Gallifreyan hierarchies. Then came some revolution, some fierce argument, some arid academic dispute, and off went the Sisterhood, to become keepers of the Flame of Eternal Life and Utter Boredom. While the universe was still less than half its present size, off to Karn went all the magic and superstition while, back on Gallifrey, science and reason gained the ascendancy. Karn grew a cult; Gallifrey grew an empire.

✑ THE DARK TIME ✑

The early Gallifreyans mounted a charge on technological advancement probably equalled – many millennia later – only by the Daleks. From simple transmat and transduction devices to the first forms of space travel and then interstellar travel, Gallifreyans spread through the cosmos like a tidal wave, or a disease. They began to encounter other life among the stars and, with that innate, unbending sense of superiority, they quickly decided that those other species needed policing. No, 'shepherding' might be more apt a description for what the Gallifreyans were up to as they built their empire. Lesser mortals were subjugated or judged too dangerous and eliminated. Gallifrey was canny, though, forming alliances – the Fledgling Empires – wherever it found powers too great to conquer.

One species, the Racnoss, derived its power from Huon energy.

The Empress of the Racnoss (above) and a Racnoss Webstar (overleaf)

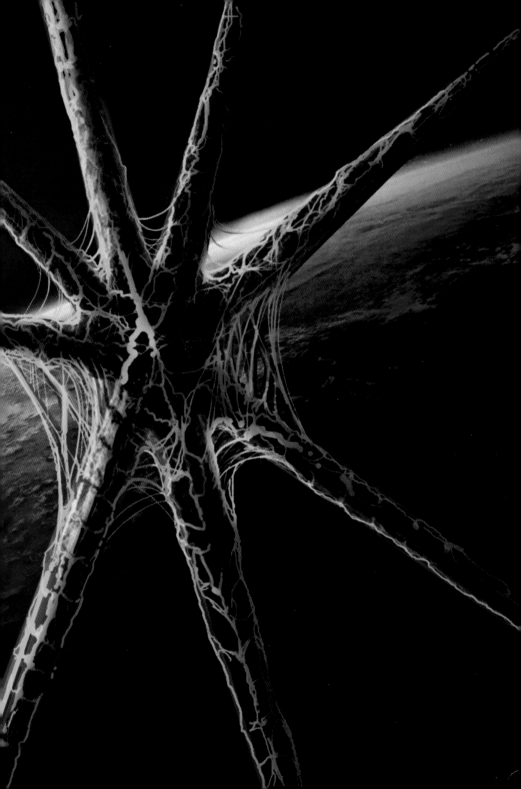

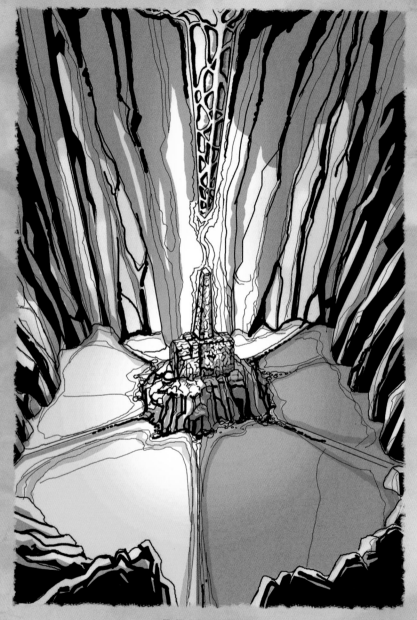

The Time Scoop game board

They were not just particularly hungry giant spiders, they were also using an energy form that unravelled the atomic structure. The Fledgling Empires went to war against the Racnoss, and the Racnoss were wiped out, more or less. One survived. (One always does.) It turned up on Earth about 4.6 billion years later, where it was cornered, drowned and burned. And the Gallifreyans got rid of Huon particles, more or less. Canny again, they quietly hung on to Huon energy, placing remnants of it at the hearts of their new travel machines. The earliest form of rudimentary time travel was born.

Well, that's one theory. Another is that it all began with the invention of the Time Scoop. (This is especially persuasive because of that pompous Time Lord way of distracting from the rubbish name with impressive capital letters. 'Huon' sings of poetry and destiny; 'Time Scoop' just sounds like a big plastic utensil.) The Time Scoop could scour the eons and snatch things out of their time, depositing them in a pentagon of barren land safely walled off by mountains – the Death Zone. Once set down, the alien creatures would fight and kill each other for the amusement of the watching Gallifreyans. As the beings they kidnapped for the Games became more and more lethal, someone decided to add an impenetrable force field, just in case.

Tremendous powers, misused disgracefully. And a tremendous opportunity for a young scientist, engineer, architect and all-round clever-clogs with an eye on politics. It's thought that Rassilon made his name on the High Council campaigning against

The Black Scrolls of Rassilon (above) and the Dark Tower in the Death Zone (overleaf)

23

the Games, and possibly his first act as President was to seal off the entire Zone and forbid the use of the Time Scoop. Note that he didn't disassemble the thing or erase it from history; he kept it hidden away in the Capitol and left a handy set of instructions called the Black Scrolls of Rassilon. Sure enough, several of his successors would uncover it – see Chapter 3.

Much, much later, the Time War put an end to any scruples about gathering up potentially useful monstrosities and depositing them in the Death Zone. The aim now, of course, was to research and develop new ways to fight the War. Which is when that official untruth about nothing ever going extinct on Gallifrey was comprehensively debunked: the resurrected Rassilon delved into the planet's prehistory, poked around in its Jurassic period and found gargantuan animals – Dinosauria. These were massive creatures, and massively destructive, and they came with their own built-in armour. Having been scooped out of their own extinction, they were experimented on and transmogrified into horrors beyond imagination.

Perhaps there's still a few of them wandering around out there.

The black hole created by Omega

ஃ THE OLD TIME ஃ

Rassilon's ascendancy coincided with Gallifrey's emergence from the Dark Time into the Old Time. It's at this point that somewhat more detailed records come into being, with Rassilon evidently keen that his preeminent role be preserved and venerated. We don't know that he wrote *The Book of the Old Time*, but we can hazard a fairly safe guess, not least because it entirely forgets to mention Omega or any other.

Omega was also on the High Council and was another renowned scientist and engineer. Together, he and Rassilon created validium, a living metal, intended to be Gallifrey's ultimate defence. They learnt fairly quickly that a sentient metal that can think for itself, tell you what it's thinking and laugh at you when you try to switch it off was not necessarily the fool-proof defensive system they'd hoped for. Establishing a pattern, they took it apart again, locked it up in a vault and totally failed to notice when it was stolen.

Meanwhile, Rassilon and Omega had been working on their time-travel theories, and calculated that to have full mastery over Time they would need a colossal energy source: to create a time field for a single sufficiently large

Omega in full protective armour

vehicle, say $5 \times (10^6)$ kilos, required 10^9 mega K-tons of power. Between them, Omega and Rassilon devised two complementary solutions.

Firstly, they theorised that the overall power requirement could be lessened if the size of the thing they wished to power could be reduced. At its simplest, if the vehicle itself were not much bigger than a cupboard on the outside, then it would need a lot less energy to move it; and if it could simultaneously be vastly larger on the inside, then it could still be used for travel, research and war. To achieve this, the real space-time event (the exterior) needed to be mapped onto a separate continuum (the interior). This was the birth of transdimensional engineering, a key Gallifreyan discovery.

The power requirement was still immense, of course. The second part of the answer lay in stellar manipulation. Detonating a star would enable them to harness the energy of the consequent supernova; the invention of black holes was no more than an interesting side effect. Omega developed a remote stellar manipulator, a powerful and sophisticated device that would allow him to detonate a star – from a safe distance. The story goes that, never shy to publicise his own achievements, Omega waved his new invention at the High Council and bellowed: 'This hand – *My Hand!* – shall be the hand that liberates our people from the Chains of Time!' At which point Rassilon, with one eye on his forthcoming memoirs, drily christened it 'the Hand of Omega'.

Sadly, Omega had got his sums wrong, and he was nothing like far enough away from the supernova he set off. He was blown into the black hole and lost in a universe of antimatter. But he left behind him the basis on which Rassilon founded Time Lord society. Plus a chance for Rassilon to get the sums right and place himself at the centre of all the histories:

Rassilon journeyed into the black void with a great fleet. Within the void, no light would shine and nothing of that outer nature continue in being, except that which existed within the Sash of Rassilon. Now Rassilon found the Eye of Harmony, which balances all things, that they may neither flux nor wither nor change their state in any measure. And he caused the Eye to be brought to the world of Gallifrey wherein he sealed this beneficence with the Great Key. Then the people rejoiced.

The Book of the Old Time

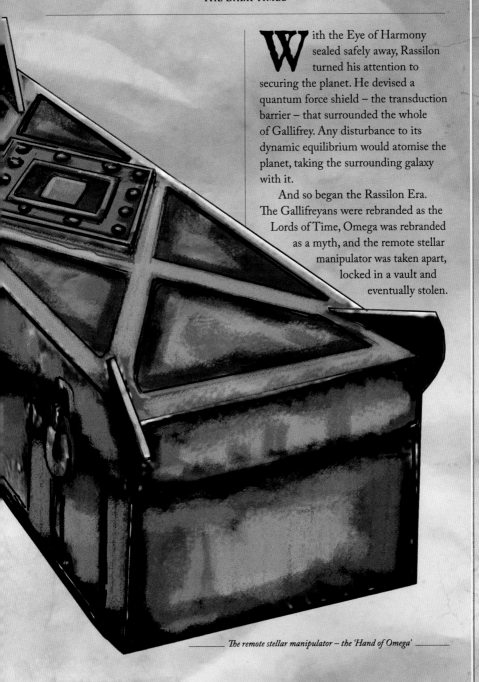

With the Eye of Harmony sealed safely away, Rassilon turned his attention to securing the planet. He devised a quantum force shield – the transduction barrier – that surrounded the whole of Gallifrey. Any disturbance to its dynamic equilibrium would atomise the planet, taking the surrounding galaxy with it.

And so began the Rassilon Era. The Gallifreyans were rebranded as the Lords of Time, Omega was rebranded as a myth, and the remote stellar manipulator was taken apart, locked in a vault and eventually stolen.

The remote stellar manipulator – the 'Hand of Omega'

ORDER FOR THE RITES OF PRESIDENTIAL INVESTITURE

Gold Usher: Honoured members of the Supreme Council, Cardinals, Time Lords. We are here today to honour the will and the wisdom of Rassilon.

All stand. Gold Usher strikes three times with his staff.

Gold Usher: Is there anyone here to contest the candidate's right to the Sash of Rassilon?

Gold Usher strikes once.

Gold Usher: Is there anyone here to contest the candidate's right to the Rod of Rassilon?

Gold Usher strikes once.

Gold Usher: Is there anyone here to contest the candidate's right to the Great Key of Rassilon?

Gold Usher strikes once.

Gold Usher: By custom, with wisdom, and for honour, I shall strike three times. Should no voice be heard by the third stroke, I will, duty-bound, invest the candidate as President of the Supreme Council of the Time Lords of Gallifrey.

Gold Usher strikes three times.

Gold Usher: It is my duty and privilege, having the consent of the Time Lords of Gallifrey, to invest you as President of the Supreme Council. Accept, therefore, the Sash of Rassilon.

The Candidate takes the Sash of Rassilon.

Gold Usher: Accept, therefore, the Rod of Rassilon.

    The Candidate takes the Rod of Rassilon.

Gold Usher: Seek, therefore, to find the Great Key of Rassilon.

    The Candidate acknowledges the Empty Cushion. *(of Rassilon)*

Gold Usher: Do you swear to uphold the Laws of Gallifrey?

Candidate: I swear.

Gold Usher: Do you swear to follow in the Wisdom of Rassilon?

Candidate: I swear.

Gold Usher: Do you swear to protect the Law and the Wisdom?

Candidate: I swear.

    The Circlet rises from the Panopticon floor.
  Gold Usher takes it and walks behind the Candidate, who kneels.

Gold Usher: I invest you Lord President of the Supreme Council.
     I wish you good fortune and strength. I give you the
     Matrix.

Gold Usher places the circlet on the President's head and moves
away. The President stands and all before him kneel.

The Sash, the Rod and the absence of the Great Key

The Rod and the Sash of Rassilon

⊱ THE ARTEFACTS OF RASSILON ⊰

E ach of the Artefacts of Rassilon was imbued with stupendous power. Whether to protect his legacy or simply to enhance his mystique, Rassilon seems to have put quite some effort into masking his technological achievements with ritual, pomp and gnomic prose. Most of the Artefacts were ceremonially bestowed upon each new President, but the purpose and meaning of them was slowly lost, their significance forgotten. Rassilon must have intended this, but he probably failed to appreciate that Time Lord society would stagnate in parallel (see Chapter 3).

We know, or can deduce, that Rassilon created the Eye of Harmony by freezing time around the exploding star then ripping that star from its orbit and suspending it in a permanent state of decay. Protected by a personal force field – the Sash of Rassilon – that prevented him being sucked into the universe of antimatter, Rassilon stabilised the black hole's nucleus and physically stored it in another vault way below the Panopticon at the heart of the Capitol, set in an eternally dynamic equation against the mass of the planet. He seems to have toyed with calling it 'Rassilon's Star' but settled on 'the Eye of Harmony', presumably for political (or poetic) reasons. (That was his last bit of restraint when it came to naming

Every TARDIS holds a subset of the Eye of Harmony

The Crown of Rassilon

The Obelisk of Rassilon

things, his reaction to Omega's stellar manipulator having quite slipped his mind.)

The Eye was sealed to prevent the forces of the black hole from pulling in the whole planet. It was controlled from a crystalline column (the Obelisk of Rassilon) set beneath the Panopticon floor. The raw Artron energy that streamed out of the Eye was siphoned off into a new generation of time-travel machines. Every travel capsule in effect contained a mathematically modelled subset of the Eye of Harmony, each splinter caught in the act of becoming a black hole. It was accessed using an ebonite rod, probably known as the Rod of Rassilon, though some accounts call it the Great Key of Rassilon.

A second device was also known as the Great Key of Rassilon, rather more fittingly since it actually was a key, not a rod. Used in conjunction with the Sash and the Rod, the Great Key would give its holder absolute power, so Rassilon decided that any President should merely 'seek' rather than hold it. Only one Time Lord President since Rassilon has held all three Artefacts – see Chapter 3.

A third device, another key, was imaginatively named the Key of Rassilon. Unlike the Crown of Rassilon, which was given to a President at the climax of his investiture, the Key of Rassilon was held by the Keeper of the Matrix. The Crown, a simple gold circlet, allowed its wearer to mentally enter the Matrix, while the Key gave

The Great Key

its user physical access, via the Seventh Door (otherwise known as the primary service hatch; pompous lot). The Matrix, of course, being the next part of Rassilon's gift to his people.

His reasoning seems to have been something like this. Any Time Lord living a full cycle of thirteen lives will have some four or five thousand years' worth of experience and knowledge: five millennia of information and expertise lost to Gallifrey every time a Time Lord dies. But what if all of it could be preserved in a database and accessed by that Time Lord's peers and successors?

The Matrix – sometimes known as the Matrix of Time – is the biggest database in history. When Time Lords die, their minds are uploaded

The Key of Rassilon is held by the Keeper of the Matrix

as amplified panotropic computations: trillions of electrochemical cells in a continuous matrix. A repository of all the information that has ever been stored, all the information that can be stored, the imprints of the personalities of almost every dead Time Lord; in a sense, a form of immortality. At the moment of death, an electrical scan is made of the brain pattern and these millions of impulses are immediately transferred to the panotropic network. The result is a living computer, whose combined knowledge and experience can predict future developments, generating prophecies out of algorithms. Its physical location is, once again, in vaults deep below the Capitol, although it can be remotely accessed from APC control units, or simply via the President's Crown. Intentionally or not, the Matrix is guarded by projections of all those dead Time Lords – the Cloister Wraiths, or Sliders. In other words, the Time Lords have got a big computer made of ghosts, in a crypt, guarded by more ghosts. Anyone mentally entering the Matrix finds themselves in a micro-

A Biog Data Extract is kept for every Time Lord

An APC Control unit

Cloister Wraiths protect the Matrix

A Confession Dial

universe, a simulated reality or a surrealist nightmare; with practice, they could also shape that environment themselves.

To give his new invention some suitably portentous gravitas, Rassilon came up with a pseudo-religious preamble to the electrical scanning process: a ritual act of purification. The Confession Dial would allow a dying Time Lord to face his demons and make his peace, before his mind was uploaded to the Matrix. (It was also a handy failsafe – it would only open if its owner was genuinely dead. Gallifreyans can take days to die, and nobody wants to wake from a late regeneration and find themselves inside a burial chamber. Or on a funeral pyre.)

Ironically, the Matrix was quite capable of generating its own portentous gravitas. One of its earliest predictions was of the fall of Gallifrey and the unravelling of the Web of Time itself. Rassilon may have tried to keep this one to himself, but in time the prophecy became a legend – the stories told of a creature, a hybrid of two great warrior races. This Hybrid would one day 'stand in the ruins of Gallifrey and destroy a billion, billion hearts to heal its own'.

But there were many stories in those times, and this one would be forgotten for billions of years.

✣ THE LAW GIVER ✣

As we have already seen, Rassilon took some care to prevent his successors equalling his own levels of power. This went beyond his standard techniques of mystification and obfuscation: he also codified his Time Lord society and its authority over Time, and laid traps for the unwary and unprincipled.

First and foremost, he established the Laws of Time. Perhaps 'established' is too strong – he was largely just describing a set of scientific principles akin to the Laws of Physics. The unintended consequence of laying down the law in this way, of course, was that it tempted so many others to break it. He said 'must not' when he meant 'cannot', although a deeper understanding than he then had might have led him to 'can, but Time will (usually) reassert itself'. Anyway, he laid down the five great principles that have been taught to every Time Lord from childhood ever since.

I swear to protect the Ancient Law of Gallifrey with all my might and main and will to the end of my days with justice and with honour temper my actions and my thoughts.

Time Lord Induction Ceremony

Rassilon also composed a rather baffling and dangerous book called *The Worshipful and Ancient Law of Gallifrey*. Baffling because it doesn't actually contain the laws of Gallifrey, per se.

The Worshipful and Ancient Law of Gallifrey

Dangerous because it was really another key. Time ran backwards over its pages, and turning its leaves in reverse order unlocked Shada, a highly secret Time Prison. Although the Time Lords started imprisoning criminals in Shada, they never actually finished building it, and it was ultimately abandoned. Like all the other Artefacts, the book's true meaning was soon forgotten and it was consigned to the Panopticon Archives, another vault deep underground, from where it was, inevitably, stolen.

When the Time Lords invented the game of chess, it may have been as part of the forbidden Games in the Death Zone – the entrance hall to the Dark Tower at the centre of the Zone boasts the gigantic Chess Board of Rassilon. ('No, try to remember, it's as easy as pi: your Drashig can only move two squares forwards then one to the side.') The Dark Tower itself was to become Rassilon's tomb when his fellow Time Lords rebelled against him and locked

The Chess Board of Rassilon

him in or, more prosaically, when he realised that his end was nigh. Either way, he made access to the Tower and its contents the final stage in a new game in the Death Zone – the Game of Rassilon. Once again, his wily paranoia made him realise that he would be followed by some who wanted to seize and misuse the power of the Time Lords. So he left clues for all the would-be dictators and demi-gods to come. The Black Scrolls of Rassilon would lead them – via the Harp of Rassilon and the accompanying Portrait of Rassilon – to a secret chamber in the Capitol, containing the controls for the Time Scoop, along with the Coronet of Rassilon, which projected and amplified its wearer's will. All this would enable any reasonably efficient power-mad conspirator to penetrate the Tower and locate the sarcophagus on which lay Rassilon's perfectly preserved body. An inscription in Old High Gallifreyan on a nearby obelisk contained the final clue:

Inside the Dark Tower

'To lose is to win, and he who wins shall lose.'

This is the Tomb of Rassilon, where Rassilon lies in eternal sleep. Anyone who has got this far has passed many dangers and shown great courage and determination. To lose is to win, and he who wins shall lose.

Whoever took the Ring of Rassilon and put it on would get the reward he sought: immortality. For Rassilon had, in fact, achieved immortality – timeless perpetual bodily regeneration – and at that time he understood that it was a curse, not a blessing. So whoever took the ring found himself trapped as a living stone image on the side of Rassilon's sarcophagus. The only shame being that Rassilon forgot all this when he was himself resurrected for the Time War. But we'll come to that much later.

THE RECORD OF RASSILON

By now the Time Lords had forsaken empire-building, and liberated most of their colonies. Throughout this period, though, and for centuries after Rassilon's time, they continued to roam through space and time, exploring and learning, teaching and influencing. As the oldest and mightiest civilisation in the universe, their interventions were frequent. They left their mark on Voga many

The Seal of Rassilon worn by an inhabitant of Voga

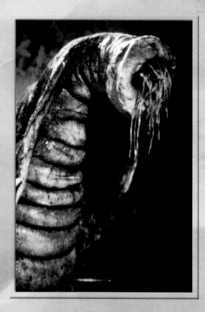

A Miniscope and a Fendahleen (top), a Sontaran and a Rutan (below)

centuries before that world was all but obliterated in the Cyber Wars. They enforced a ban on Miniscopes, devices which, ironically, functioned in much the same way as Gallifreyan painting, if more primitive – a slice of real space preserved, rather than a slice of real time frozen. They were rumoured to have arbitrated unsuccessfully in the endless war between the Rutans and the Sontarans. They attempted to destroy the phenomenally lethal Fendahl, time-looping its entire planet (originally Sol Five in Mutter's Spiral). And, on occasion, they went to war.

When a race of giant vampires appeared out of nowhere and swarmed across the universe, Rassilon led the hunt for them. The creatures were so strong that one single vampire could suck the life out of an entire planet. According to *The Record of Rassilon*, 'Energy weapons were useless because the monsters absorbed and transmuted the energy, using it to become stronger. Therefore Rassilon ordered the construction of Bowships: swift vessels that fired a mighty bolt of steel that transfixed the monsters through the heart. For only if his heart be utterly destroyed will a vampire die.' *The Record of Rassilon* was an emergency instruction installed in all time vehicles of the period:

The Great Vampire

So powerful were the bodies of these great creatures, and so fiercely did they cling to life, that they were impossible to kill, save by the use of Bowships. Yet slain they all were, and to the last one, by the Lords of Time, the Lords of Time destroying them utterly. However, when the bodies were counted, the King Vampire, mightiest and most malevolent of all, had vanished, even to his shadow, from time and space. Hence it is the directive of Rassilon that any Time Lord who comes upon this enemy of our people and of all living things, shall use all his efforts to destroy him, even at the cost of his own life.

The Record of Rassilon

The Time Lords hunted the vampires down across the universe in a war so long and so bloody that they were sickened of violence for ever, or so went the propaganda. Soon after, Rassilon retreated – or was pushed – into his Tomb. There was no longer any public or political appetite for war, and it would take only one more crisis to push Gallifrey into a state of isolationism.

A Minyan ion-drive starship

That crisis came when the Time Lords visited the planet Minyos. The primitive Minyans thought of the Time Lords as gods. The visitors gave Minyos medical and scientific aid, communications technology and better weapons. The Minyans kicked the Time Lords out at gunpoint, then went to war with each other, learnt how to split the atom, and finally split the planet. All that was left of the Minyan civilisation was contained in a couple of ion-drive starships, which fled to the other side of the universe.

The Minyos disaster led directly and almost immediately to the Time Lords' policy of non-intervention.

CHAPTER TWO

GALACTIC TICKET INSPECTORS

A ny good oligarchy will always operate on the principle of getting the difficult bit out of the way in the title. Staying out of other races' business was all very well, but there was a constant risk of other, less enlightened beings developing time-travel technology and misusing it terribly. Best, then, to act quickly to stamp out unlicensed time travel. So the legalistic waffle that constitutes the Law of Non-Interference in the Affairs of Other Planets actually manages a fair few sidesteps, not least in the discreet founding of the Celestial Intervention Agency. The purpose of the CIA, in its simplest form, was to maintain the Time Lords' profile across space and time, pursuing Gallifrey's best interests while leaving everyone back home with the contented belief that they only observed and never interfered.

Well, nearly everyone back home. There were a fair few renegades, evildoers

Intervening across space and time

and do-gooders, and we'll come to some of them in Chapter 4. Most of them tended to be hauled back in and punished, though a brief skim through the relevant court records suggests that what really irritated the authorities was (a) the overt flouting of the Law and (b) a general failure to fill in the correct forms before doing the flouting. The punishment for unauthorised absence from Gallifrey, more often than not, was being sent away from Gallifrey, in much the same way as a Level Five civilisation

The Doctor absconds in a faulty TT capsule

will tend to execute people who've attempted suicide.

This is well illustrated by a case study: the Doctor, partly because we have to get to him sooner or later, but mostly because he supplied the title for this chapter. Every Time Tot knows how the story goes: claiming that he was bored with our immensely civilised lifestyle of observation and information-gathering, he stole a faulty time-travel capsule, fled Gallifrey and started careering around the cosmos, righting wrongs, defeating monsters and abducting Humans. Eventually, we caught up with him, gave him a slap on the wrist and sent him out again to right wrongs, defeat monsters and abduct Humans. Occasionally, he would pop back home, generally bringing some

disaster with him, but that was about the size of it until the Time War.

That there's a little more to it than that is indicated by what he took with him when he absconded: a faulty Type 40 TT capsule; the validium; the Hand of Omega; the President's daughter; and Gallifrey's moon (although in fairness he claims that he didn't steal the moon, he just lost it). He didn't leave because he was bored; he left because he was scared. What was he scared of? A ghost story? The Time Lords? Himself? Someone should ask him some day. But let's say that, in his own muddled way, he was scared of what *he* might do with all of Gallifrey's power, and so he was scared of what *anyone* might do with it. Off he went, taking any of Gallifrey's most dangerous technology that wasn't nailed

The Doctor on trial

down and wouldn't be missed for a while. That doesn't quite hang together yet, but it may be inching towards the truth.

Out he went, into the universe, using a fraction of his powers in battle with cruel Dominators and deadly Quarks, lethal robot Yeti, brutal Martians, relentless Cybermen and pitiless Daleks. He made a vow to himself always to help those in need, never to be cruel or cowardly, never giving up, never giving in. (Yes, he was a boyhood hero of mine.) And he sacrificed his own freedom when faced with the task of returning thousands of kidnapped Humans to different time zones in Earth's history – having no way to get them all home in his TARDIS, with its defective navigational systems, he called in the Time Lords.

AGENCY AGENT

Strangely, the authorities decided not to make a public example of him. A Malfeasance Tribunal dealt with him in closed session and, through the intercession of the CIA, accepted his argument that there were times when intervention was necessary. Or, to put it another way, the tribunal recognised that he'd broken official Time Lord policy but was actually enacting unofficial official Time Lord policy, so they might as well let him get on with it. The court transcripts eventually released conclude with the tribunal sentencing the Doctor to exile in one time zone on one planet and an enforced regeneration from his second into his third incarnation:

Some of the evils the Doctor fought against

TRIBUNAL We have accepted your plea that there is evil in the universe that must be fought, and that you still have a part to play in that battle.

DEFENDANT What? You mean that you're going to let me go free?

TRIBUNAL Not entirely. We have noted your particular interest in the planet Earth. The frequency of your visits must have given you special knowledge of that world and its problems.

DEFENDANT Yes, I suppose that's true. Earth seems more vulnerable than others, yes.

TRIBUNAL For that reason, you will be sent back to that planet.

DEFENDANT Oh, good.

TRIBUNAL In exile.

DEFENDANT In exile?

TRIBUNAL You will be sent to Earth in the twentieth century, and will remain there for as long as we deem proper, and for that period the secret of the TARDIS will be taken from you.

DEFENDANT But you can't condemn me to exile on one primitive planet in one century in time! Besides, I'm known on the Earth. It might be very awkward for me.

TRIBUNAL Your appearance has changed before, it will change again. That is part of the sentence.

Malfeasance Tribunal 309906

There are suggestions, however, that the Doctor was removed from the courtroom before the regeneration process could be started. The Doctor had been recruited as a CIA agent; it was the price he paid for his freedom.

This second life for his second life seems to have been relatively brief, and was conceivably curtailed by the disaster at Space Station J7, designated *Camera*. The CIA had been monitoring the temporal experiments of two Third

Joinson Dastari

Zone professors, Kartz and Reimer, and had detected ripples of up to 0.4 on the Bocher scale. Since anything much higher would threaten the whole fabric of time, the CIA wanted the experiments halted. The Doctor was duly despatched to confront Joinson Dastari, Head of Projects. Within minutes, Space Station *Camera* was under attack from the Ninth Sontaran Battle Group. Almost the whole Station staff was slaughtered, and computer records were falsified to attribute blame to the Time Lords. Dastari, a pioneer in genetic engineering, was working for or with the Sontarans, and planned to isolate the symbiotic nuclei of a Time Lord in the hope of gaining the secret of time travel.

It seems likely that the carnage at Space Station *Camera* forced the CIA to cover up their ongoing use of the Doctor. The original sentence of the tribunal was enforced, and the Doctor regenerated and began his exile on Earth. There is no doubt, however, that within a few months he was again acting on instructions from the Agency. They initially made contact with him when they discovered that the Master had also arrived on twentieth-century Earth (see Chapter 4), but this seems to

A Group Marshal of the Ninth Sontaran Battle Group

The Master

The ancient Chronovore Kronos

have involved little more than a friendly warning. Not long afterwards, though, the Doctor's exile was temporarily rescinded.

The Master had broken into the Matrix files, extracting data on the ancient Chronovores, Earth's *Homo reptilia*, the Dæmons of Dæmos, and the Doomsday Weapon developed on the planet Uxarieus. This last posed the greatest immediate threat: the Doomsday Weapon could force a sun to burn through to its core and explode in an instant. In possession of the Doomsday Weapon, the Master would be able to hold entire galaxies to ransom, threatening tens of billions of years' worth of lives. The Doctor was duly sent to Uxarieus.

Further assignments followed. The accession of the planet Peladon

Homo reptilia

A Dæmon

The Guardian of the Doomsday Weapon

The citadel of Peladon

Aggedor

to the Galactic Federation in the late thirty-ninth century was identified as a crucial event in the history of the universe, and the Agency had identified a conspiracy to prevent it, so they sent in the Doctor. He uncovered a collaboration between Peladon's xenophobic High Priest, Hepesh, and a delegate from the planet Arcturus. Together, they were assassinating members of the court and Federation delegates using the Royal Beast of Peladon, Aggedor. Hepesh hoped to stimulate Peladon's natural tendency to superstition and so increase his own power; Arcturus hoped to secure the planet's extensive trisilicate reserves for his own world.

Galactic Federation delegates from the planet Mars

A key stage in the retrenchment of Earth's thirtieth-century empire was the decolonisation of the planet Solos. Earth's Marshal on Solos, however, ruling the planet from an orbiting space station, not only opposed Earth's plans but also intended to commit genocide against the native people, using the excuse that the Solonians were mutating into creatures dubbed Mutts. Only the Time Lords were aware that this mutant phase was a natural part of the Solonian life cycle, which had been accelerated by the occupying Earth forces' atmospheric experiments. There was a series of four adaptive changes in the indigenous population every five hundred years over a two-thousand-year sequence, culminating in the evolution of a highly gifted super-being. The Doctor was despatched to Solos.

FREE AGENT

Sooner or later, the Doctor was going to refuse one of these missions – he was after all being bounced back to twentieth-century Earth at the end of each one, like a galactic yo-yo, and his third incarnation was proving considerably more bad-tempered about it all than his second. So it seemed a good idea to give him back his freedom, in the hope that he would remain reasonably cooperative and compliant.

The opportunity to 'reward' the Doctor in this way came quickly

and from an unexpected direction – the discovery that Omega had not, after all, perished in the black hole he'd created (see Chapter 1). He had instead become the mad king of an antimatter world, and now intended to return to corporeal form in our universe. He instigated a catastrophic drain of cosmic energy from Gallifrey into the black hole. The Time Lords' time-travel facility was soon in danger, but that was only the beginning. If the energy drain continued, then eventually the whole fabric of space-time would be destroyed.

Powerless to help themselves, the Time Lords turned again to the Doctor. On the direct orders of the President, and despite objections from the Chancellor, Gallifrey itself broke the First Law of Time, using time-scoop technology to extract the first two Doctors from their time streams and unite them with the third in the battle against Omega. The three Doctors succeeded, apparently destroying Omega, reversing the energy drain and providing – in the detonation of the antimatter universe – a new power source for Gallifrey.

A Mutt

Omega

PRESIDENT Is the Doctor holding out?

TECHNICIAN We are giving his TARDIS all the energy we can spare.

PRESIDENT And the hostile?

TECHNICIAN Unidentified so far, my lord.

CHANCELLOR And the source of this beam?

PRESIDENT You see, Chancellor? The black hole.

CHANCELLOR That's a nowhere… no place, a void. According to all known laws, nothing can exist there.

PRESIDENT Yet somehow, through this black hole, vital cosmic energy is draining away in spite of all we can do to check it.

TECHNICIAN Already the time-travel facility is in danger, my lord.

PRESIDENT Without it, we shall be helpless. Unless the energy loss is stopped the whole fabric of space time will be destroyed. We are being consumed and we can find no way to fight back.

CHANCELLOR Are you telling me we are up against an adversary, a force, equal to our own?

PRESIDENT Equal and *opposite* to our own.

CHANCELLOR A force which inhabits a universe where by definition even we cannot exist?

PRESIDENT Yes. A force in the universe of antimatter.

CHANCELLOR But that's too terrible to contemplate. Someone must go and help the Doctor.

PRESIDENT I agree, but no one can be spared, your excellency. Everyone is needed to combat the energy drain.

CHANCELLOR Are you saying we can't help him?

PRESIDENT Yes, I am… But perhaps he can help himself. Show me the Doctor's time stream, the section for his earlier self before he changed his form.

CHANCELLOR You can't allow him to cross his own time stream. Apart from the enormous energy it would need, the First Law of Time expressly forbids him to meet his other selves.

PRESIDENT I am aware of that, your excellency, but this is an emergency.

CHANCELLOR But you can't!

PRESIDENT Your excellency, I have to.

CHANCELLOR Be it on your own head.

Official minutes

The Doctor's knowledge of time-travel law was now restored and his Earth exile was remitted. The CIA, meanwhile, stepped back into the shadows, at least for a time, conscious perhaps that their semi-regular employment of the Doctor had come close to being discovered at the highest levels of Time Lord society. Their only contact with the Doctor for the remainder of his third incarnation came when he asked for their help in tracking down a Dalek army and averting an intergalactic war. Even then, they did the bare minimum, merely guiding his TARDIS to the planet Spiridon and leaving him to face the massed ranks of 10,000 Daleks.

A Matrix projection ended their reticence. It predicted a time when the Daleks would have destroyed all other life forms and become the dominant creature in the universe. It was decided to return the Doctor, now in his fourth life, to the Dalek home world, Skaro, at a point in time just before the creatures evolved. In theory, the Doctor might be able to affect their genetic development so that they evolved into less aggressive creatures; at the very least, he might uncover some inherent weakness that would make them easier to overcome. Or he could actually avert their creation. Despite his qualms, the Doctor accepted the mission.

He failed completely. Not only that, but the law of unintended consequences kicked in. Until the Doctor's arrival, Davros, the creator of the Daleks, had concluded that

The Doctor is sent to avert the creation of the Daleks...

... but does he have the right?

Morbius

Skaro was the only planet in the seven galaxies known to him that was capable of supporting intelligent life. The Doctor's presence proved him wrong, and Davros quickly recognised that his Daleks must have a far more significant future than he had so far imagined, if aliens from the future were trying to interfere at their birth. His ambitions for his Daleks now moved swiftly from the conquest of Skaro to the subjugation of the entire universe. By deploying the Doctor against the embryonic Daleks, the CIA may have managed to light the spark that would eventually blaze through creation as the Last Great Time War.

That war, though, was a long way into the future, too far off for even a Matrix prophecy. So the CIA now continued as before, still occasionally calling on the Doctor's services. On leaving Skaro, the Doctor found himself fighting a Cyberman attempt to destroy the last remnant of Voga. And when relations soured between the Time Lords and the Sisterhood of Karn, with their leader Maren declaring their alliance at an end and supplies of the Elixir of Life seemingly drying up, the Doctor's TARDIS was diverted.

Landing on Karn, he learnt that the Sacred Flame was apparently dying and the Elixir of Life was not forming. The flame was the product of gases forcing up along a geological fault from deep in the molten heart of the planet. The heat from the flame caused

Davros and his evil creation

oxidation of the chemicals in the rocks that led to to a chemical reaction with the rising superheated gases, producing the Elixir. The Doctor deduced that a subterranean tremor had sealed in the gases, preventing the flame from forming.

The Doctor easily freed the trapped gases. What nobody expected was to find that one of Gallifrey's greatest war criminals had survived execution by the Time Lords. The brain of Morbius had been preserved after his body was atomised in a dispersal chamber. His living mind had remained, shielded, on Karn for years (see Chapter 4). The CIA probably saw the Doctor's presence on Karn as a case of serendipity, and may well have been drawing up plans to increase their use of this free agent.

Then crisis struck Gallifrey again.

CHAPTER THREE

A STATE OF DECAY

While the Celestial Intervention Agency went quietly about its affairs, monitoring and meddling across time and space as it saw fit, Time Lord society entered a phase of rapid atrophy. For millennia, the Time Lords of Gallifrey led a life of peace and ordered calm, apparently protected from all threats or intrusions from lesser civilisations. They continued to observe and record, debate and philosophise,

thousands of elderly men pottering through their ancient records largely for the sake of pottering through their ancient records. With no motivation to improve themselves or help others, they declined into an impotent race that had forgotten quite how much power it could wield.

Now rarely venturing from Gallifrey, the Time Lords turned aside from the 'barren road' of technology; any research and development now going on, like the new Time Rings, was pretty much down to the CIA. The majority of the Time Lords simply forgot that they were, quite literally, sitting right on top of one of the greatest feats of engineering the universe had ever known. They forgot the functions of Rassilon's Artefacts, dismissing them as having no more than symbolic value. When a new President was invested, he was handed the symbols of office, a succession of

A Time Ring

The Lord High President – no different from any other Time Lord?

Rassilonian grandeur

technological masterpieces, yet he was viewed as nothing more than an elected figurehead, no different from any other Time Lord. Ceremonial robes became everyday dress. The Time Lords even stopped noticing the majestic architecture that Rassilon had left them, slowly replacing it with drably functional decors, fixtures and fittings. By the end of the Borusa presidency, the Capitol's splendour had been reduced to the unappetising pallor of a spaceport lounge.

The Time Lords' general inertia in this period left them wide open to political machinations and even outside attack. It was a combination of the two that led to the Borusa presidency that bookends and defines this period.

It's worth rehearsing the official history of the initial events here. A renegade Time Lord known as the Master arrived on Gallifrey to assassinate the 406th President of the High Council of Gallifrey on Presidential Resignation Day. The deceased President's Resignation Honours List had, as expected, named the Chancellor, Goth, as his successor. Goth heroically tracked down the assassin and killed him, unfortunately perishing himself in the exchange of staser fire. Borusa, a much-admired tutor at the Academy only recently elevated

Gallifreyan architecture and design…

... its mysterious splendour...

... and its decline and fall

to the position of Cardinal, became Chancellor and Acting President by popular acclaim until he could be confirmed as President by election.

That's what it says in the Bureau of Ancient Records. And not one word of it is true. This is the truth:

The renegade Time Lord known as the Master, having reached the end of his twelfth and final regeneration, was dying on Tersurus, one of the Outer Planets, where he was discovered by Chancellor Goth. The Master promised Goth power and knowledge in exchange for a lift back to Gallifrey, where he intended to regenerate himself using the energy of the Eye of Harmony. On the Master's behalf, Goth accessed the Matrix through an APC Control unit and sent a telepathic summons to the Doctor, intending to use him as a scapegoat for the killing of the President. Goth later claimed that he was unable to fight the Master's mental dominance, but he seems primarily to have been motivated by the prospect of power: he is on record as admitting that the outgoing President had told him that – despite widespread expectations – he would not be named as successor in the Resignation Honours List. Willingly or otherwise, Goth concealed a staser in his Chancellor's robes of state and fired on his victim at close range, colluding with the Master to frame the Doctor for the assassination.

Chancellor Goth kneels over his victim

The Doctor is arrested for the President's murder

HILRED You will confess, Doctor.

THE DOCTOR All right, all right, I'll confess.

HILRED Very sensible.

THE DOCTOR I confess you're a bigger idiot than I thought you were. Aargh!

HILRED There are fifteen intensity levels in this device, Doctor. At the moment, you're only experiencing Level 9. Much easier to talk.

THE DOCTOR I've got nothing to say.

HILRED Oh, you'll think of something, soon.

THE DOCTOR Dum dum.

SPANDRELL Turn it off.

THE DOCTOR Tweedledee?

SPANDRELL I must apologise for my subordinate. He lets his enthusiasm run away with him.

THE DOCTOR I see. The hot and cold technique.

SPANDRELL We are simply seekers of the truth, and we haven't got much time. Chancellor Goth has ordered your immediate trial.

THE DOCTOR I'd like to help you. How about a signed confession?

SPANDRELL That will help. I hate going to court without possessing the full facts. Motive, for instance.

THE DOCTOR Now that's a sensible question. Why should anyone want to assassinate a retiring President?

SPANDRELL A personal grudge?

THE DOCTOR I never met him.

SPANDRELL I know. I have seen your biog.

THE DOCTOR And you still think I did it? ☞

SPANDRELL I think you're going to be executed for it. They are preparing the vaporisation chamber now. You have about three hours to live, Doctor.

THE DOCTOR What? That's monstrous. Vaporisation without representation is against the Constitution.

SPANDRELL You are an embarrassment.

THE DOCTOR You realise I've been framed, don't you?

SPANDRELL Framed?

THE DOCTOR Yes, framed. It's an Earth expression. It means that someone's gone to a great deal of trouble to get me into this mess.

SPANDRELL Why did you come back here?

THE DOCTOR To try and save the President's life. If you remember, I left a note for you.

SPANDRELL Yes.

THE DOCTOR Which, presumably, you did nothing about.

SPANDRELL All that I could. So you knew the President was going to be assassinated?

THE DOCTOR Yes. In a way, I experienced it.

SPANDRELL Go on.

THE DOCTOR Well, this is the bit you won't believe. People talk of a premonition of tragedy, but I actually saw it happening. I saw the President die as vividly, as clearly as I can see this room now.

SPANDRELL And where were you when this happened?

THE DOCTOR In the TARDIS, travelling in Vortex, after I'd heard the Panopticon summons.

Transcript of the interrogation
of the Doctor by
Castellan Spandrell and
Commander Hilred

The Master at the end of his lives

The Doctor's trial

Chancellor Goth perished from psychosomatic feedback while again accessing the Matrix. The Doctor prevented the Master from opening the Eye of Harmony and regenerating himself, and the Master escaped in a hidden TARDIS. The partial opening of the Eye left half the Capitol in ruins, with countless deaths among the damage. Cardinal Borusa decreed that the truth should be adjusted for the public good. The story was rewritten to make Goth a public hero and leave the Doctor's role unmentioned and disregarded. The Doctor was politely asked to leave Gallifrey and happily did so. What neither he nor Borusa appreciated at that point was that his departure would leave the Time Lords in a constitutional crisis.

The High Council ratified Borusa's appointment as Chancellor, and he presumably intended to stand for the presidency. Unfortunately for him, this proved legally impossible. In the immediate aftermath of the previous President's death, the Doctor had been arrested and tried for the assassination. Spotting a legal loophole, he had declared himself a candidate for the presidency and invoked Article 17 of the Constitution:

No candidate for office shall in any way be debarred or restrained from presenting his claim.

The previous President had died without naming his successor, and the Constitution demanded that an election be held within forty-eight hours. With Goth's death, there was no other legitimate candidate – the Doctor became the 407th President of the Time Lords by default. In the President's absence, and realising that the one thing it didn't have was supreme authority, the High Council renamed itself the Supreme Council. It then wriggled its way around the technicalities and nominated Chancellor Borusa as Acting President. Everyone settled down and looked forward to a few decades of legal wrangling and point-scoring. The one thing they were all certain of was that the Doctor would not return to assume the position of President.

Then the Doctor returned to assume the position of President.

THE INVASIONS OF GALLIFREY

The Time Lords are a race of great technical achievement, but lacking the morale to withstand a determined assault.

Sontaran Military Intelligence Appreciation: GALLIFREY

Aside from his brief appearance before the Malfeasance Tribunal, the Doctor's entanglement in the Master's attack had seen his only return to Gallifrey since he first absconded, several centuries earlier. He obviously wasn't impressed by what he saw.

Later, stumbling on the Vardans and their plan to invade Gallifrey, perhaps he judged that there were too many venal and self-serving Time Lords who'd prove only too willing to help out the would-be conquerors – that the 'traitor' might as well be someone who'd actually try to fight back. Or did he just reckon the Time Lords needed shaking out of their complacency, gambling everything on his own capacity singlehandedly to save the day?

Either way, the Doctor opened a window into the Capitol and let the Vardans in. Realising that he was the de facto President just made it all that bit easier. Once inaugurated, the Doctor allowed a small force of Vardans through the transduction barrier and introduced the Supreme Council to their 'new masters'. Few resisted, many complied, and a few actively helped their conquerors. Foremost among these was Kelner, the current Castellan, who may have hoped to replace the Doctor as the Vardans' puppet President. With the Constitution suspended, Time Lords loyal to 'the old ways' were rounded up and banished into the Drylands.

The Doctor's investiture as Lord High President

Castellan Kelner colluded with the Vardan and Sontaran invaders

PRESIDENT   Gentlemen, this is no ordinary meeting. I'm privileged to introduce to you your new masters.

CHANCELLOR   He's mad! Guard!

PRESIDENT   Resistance is useless. The Vardans have more power than we have dreamed of and more knowledge than we can hope for. You must submit, the way I did when I first met them.

CHANCELLOR   And when was that?

PRESIDENT   A long time ago.

CHANCELLOR   So you knew about this all the time. You knew about this before your induction.

PRESIDENT   Yes, before that, yes.

CHANCELLOR   And all you know is in the Matrix.

PRESIDENT   And all I know is in the Matrix.

CHANCELLOR   You really disappoint me, Doctor. I expected better of you.

PRESIDENT   Did you really? Thank you. You will now disperse until my next summons.

Minutes of extraordinary meeting of the Supreme Council

All this was a sideshow. The Vardans travelled along any form of broadcast wavelength. As soon as their spearhead fully materialised, the Doctor was able to identify their planet of origin and activate a modulation rejection pattern. He sent the invaders back to their home world then time-looped it. Clever, if reckless.

Not quite clever enough, though. What the Doctor did not know was that the Vardans were nothing more than an expendable advance guard. Having opened a hole in the transduction barrier, the Doctor had actually let in shock troops from the Sontaran Special Space Service. Their aim was to seize the Rod, the Sash and the Great Key of Rassilon, the three together – when linked into the Matrix – providing the sum total of Time Lord power. If successful, the Sontarans could rampage through all times in all universes.

This time there was no pretence at cooperation with the invaders. Kelner, scared for his own life, helped them, but the Doctor led the counter-attack. He persuaded Chancellor Borusa to reveal the location of the Great Key and used it to construct a De-mat Gun. An ultimate weapon from the Dark Time, it enabled the Doctor to delete the entire Sontaran force.

ONCE AGAIN, OMEGA

The Doctor gave up the Presidency before leaving Gallifrey again, and Chancellor Borusa was formally invested as President, the Supreme Council reverting to just 'High' in the process. Borusa had witnessed the wisdom of Rassilon first hand: the Doctor had been the first President since Rassilon to hold the Sash, the Rod and the Great Key, but the memory of all this had been somehow stripped

Lord President Borusa and his Inner Council

from him at the moment he used the De-mat Gun. Borusa seems to have undergone a self-induced regeneration at this stage, perhaps acknowledging his responsibility to forget what he knew.

Unhappily, his next incarnation proved quite ineffectual, and he presided over a High Council rife with plotting and manoeuvring for political advantage. His first Chancellor, Thalia, was just as unimpressive, as was Cardinal Zorac. President Borusa decided to raise the Castellan to High Council status, replacing Kelner at the same time. The new Castellan was not a team player, however, overtly courting public popularity with more hard-line policies than his President. This left only Councillor Hedin – a man of learning with centuries of public service, respected by all – as a calming voice of reason when Gallifrey faced its next crisis. Unfortunately, that crisis was precipitated by Hedin himself.

Hedin had made contact with a legendary figure from Gallifrey's ancient history. Omega had not, after all, been killed in the destruction of his antimatter universe (see Chapter 2). He continued to exist in antimatter form, and remained obsessed with returning to our universe. Now utterly unhinged and (rightly) blaming the Doctor for his earlier defeat, the physical form he planned to take was the Doctor's fifth body. For his part, Hedin saw only the first and greatest of our people, the one who sacrificed all to give us mastery of Time and was shamefully abandoned in

Omega bonded with the Doctor

return. The Councillor stole the Doctor's biodata from the Matrix, enabling Omega to effect a temporal bonding with the Doctor and achieve physical form.

Borusa's fallible judgement was plainly revealed during this emergency. It was patently obvious that the only way for Omega to have procured the Doctor's biodata extract was through a traitor on the High Council. Despite this, the President led the majority of the High Council in sentencing the Doctor to execution in an effort to prevent the temporal bonding. From within the Matrix, Omega ensured that the Doctor survived the termination, though this almost inevitably led to his own final defeat.

Omega and his disciple, Councillor Hedin

PRESIDENT This session of the High Council of Time Lords is now in progress. The space-time parameters of the Matrix have been invaded by a creature from the antimatter world. We know its composition and how unstable is the magnetism that shields it. The creature must be expelled immediately if we are to avert disaster.

THE DOCTOR Without knowing its purpose here.

PRESIDENT Its presence here must be our first concern. Antimatter cannot coexist in harmony in our universe.

THE DOCTOR Lord President, this creature is here now because it bonded with me. To do so it needed something very special, full and precise details of my biological makeup. Now, I didn't pass this information on. Somebody did. The question is who.

CASTELLAN We considered this, Doctor, but the implications are quite preposterous.

THE DOCTOR Chancellor, can bonding occur without the full imprint of a so-called bio-scan?

CHANCELLOR Not to my knowledge. But the power of this creature is outside the limits of what we know, Doctor.

THE DOCTOR Lord President, I ask for time to have this fully investigated.

PRESIDENT I'm sorry, Doctor, but we must deal with the situation as it exists now. The time factor involved leaves only one course of action open to us. Commander! You know that capital punishment has long been abolished here in Gallifrey, but there is a precedent for a situation like this. Have you nothing further to say, Doctor?

THE DOCTOR   I have a great deal to say.

NYSSA OF TRAKEN   You can't do this. You must destroy the creature.

PRESIDENT   Child, do you think we have not considered this? The creature is shielded. We have no way of tracing it.

NYSSA OF TRAKEN   So you're prepared to kill the Doctor?

PRESIDENT   Commander! Remove the Doctor to the security compound. As soon as the warrant is issued, you will convey him to a place of termination. I'm sorry, Doctor.

NYSSA OF TRAKEN   No! You can't!

THE DOCTOR   Executing me will not alter the fact there's a traitor at work on Gallifrey!

Transcript of emergency session of the High Council

The Doctor's companion, Nyssa of Traken, addresses the High Council

The Tomb of Rassilon

Borusa's ultimate fate

PRESIDENT ETERNAL

Soon after these events, President Borusa regenerated again. His new incarnation was considerably more formidable, with even the Castellan publicly noting his stubbornness. As it turned out, his new incarnation was also considerably more unbalanced. Having ruled Gallifrey, openly or from behind the scenes, for so long, Borusa now saw only limits to what he could achieve before he would be forced to retire. As his thoughts turned to his legacy, he

pondered another legacy – Rassilon's. Perhaps his presidential Matrix access gave him the clues, or perhaps a chance discovery of the Black Scrolls of Rassilon pointed the way. Whatever the route, Borusa found himself plotting an audacious scheme to secure immortality and rule Gallifrey for ever.

Having determined that Rassilon's secret lay – with Rassilon – in the Dark Tower, Borusa reactivated the Death Zone. He needed someone to get through the Zone and gain access to the Tower for him. Initially, he seems to have tried using High

Council members, sending in both Chancellor Thalia and Cardinal Zorac on the pretext of an investigation into the cause of an energy drain from the Eye of Harmony into the Zone. But with the Zone operational, its many traps were also sprung, and the two councillors were probably killed within moments of going in. Concluding that he would need someone rather more resourceful to reach his goal, Borusa used the forbidden Time Scoop to remove five incarnations of the Doctor from their time streams and place them in the Death Zone. He also endeavoured to cover his tracks by providing the Doctors with a number of old enemies to fight inside the Zone.

The Harp of Rassilon

CASTELLAN He has arrived.

PRESIDENT Involving this person does not please me.

CASTELLAN The Constitution clearly states that when, in emergency session, the members of the Inner Council are unanimous—

CHANCELLOR —which indeed we are—

PRESIDENT —the President of the Council may be overruled. What a ridiculous clause. Very well, have him enter.

CASTELLAN With all due respect, Lord President, your regeneration has not helped your stubbornness.

THE MASTER Lord President, Castellan, Chancellor Flavia. This is a very great and, may I say, a most unexpected honour. I may be seated? Now then, what can I do for you?

PRESIDENT You are one of the most evil and corrupt beings this Time Lord race has ever produced. Your crimes are without number and your villainy without end. Nevertheless, we are prepared to offer you a full and free pardon.

THE MASTER What makes you think I want your forgiveness?

CASTELLAN We can offer you an alternative to your renegade existence.

PRESIDENT Regeneration. A complete new life cycle.

THE MASTER What must I do?

PRESIDENT Rescue the Doctor.

THE MASTER What?

PRESIDENT The Death Zone.

THE MASTER Ah, the black secret at the heart of your Time Lord paradise. ☞

CASTELLAN Recently, the Zone has become reactivated. Somehow, it is draining energy from the Eye of Harmony—

CHANCELLOR —to an extent which endangers all Gallifrey.

PRESIDENT We must know what is happening there.

THE MASTER Did it occur to you to go and look?

PRESIDENT Two of the High Council went into the Zone. Neither returned.

THE MASTER So you sent for the Doctor?

CASTELLAN We looked for the Doctor, but he no longer exists. Not in any of his regenerations.

PRESIDENT The Doctor has been taken out of time.

Minutes of meeting of the Inner Council

It was a good call, inasmuch as the combined Doctors did indeed reach and breach the Dark Tower and locate Rassilon's tomb. Once there, they lowered the force field surrounding the Zone, and Borusa was able to transmat into the Tower to claim his prize. Borusa, it transpired, was merely the latest in an ignominious line of Time Lords seeking eternal life. His consciousness was at least the fourth to be imprisoned within a stone image on the side of Rassilon's sarcophagus (see Chapter 1).

The loss of Borusa left a gap at the very summit of the Time Lord hierarchy. With breathtaking disregard for the lessons of history, the High Council exercised its emergency powers to appoint the Doctor to the position of President, to take office immediately. When the then Chancellor, Flavia, informed him of his new position, the Doctor – being the Doctor – gave her full deputy powers and promptly fled in his TARDIS. The resulting constitutional crisis would have far-reaching consequences.

Chancellor Flavia confers the presidency on the Doctor

DECADENCE & DEGENERATION

As you probably expect by now, the official records skirt round much of what happened next. It is known that the High Council declared that, since he was wilfully neglecting the responsibility of his great office, the Doctor could be deposed. There are stories of Flavia combining the offices of Chancellor and President, and of revolts against her and her High Council, possibly even with the collusion of the CIA. One unlikely myth even involves Borusa making an unexpected return from the living dead to unite Gallifrey once more.

Whatever the truth of those times, what can be established beyond doubt is that ongoing instability at the top left Gallifrey increasingly vulnerable. Until now, only rogue Time Lords had been responsible for the ever-growing list of things stolen from Gallifrey. Around this time, though, a metamorphic symbiosis regenerator (used by Time Lords in cases of acute regenerative crisis) was appropriated by a small group of non-Gallifreyan scientists. The implications of this petty case of breaking and entering were too embarrassing to be entered into the official histories, of course. Which is a shame, because someone in authority might have been forced to do something to stop it happening again.

Instead, Gallifrey remained open to infiltration.

Three Andromedans found a way to break into the Matrix and steal scientific secrets from the Time Lords. They continued undetected for several years, operating from Earth rather than Andromeda because they assumed that the Time Lords would eventually trace the leak. When they did, the High Council ordered the use of a Magnatron to relocate the planet Earth and its entire constellation a couple of light years across space. This caused a fireball which nearly destroyed the planet, but Earth survived as 'Ravalox'. The pilfered secrets were buried deep underground on this 'new' world, and Gallifrey's secrets were safe. Ish.

Ravalox became a celebrated scientific and astronomical curiosity since the planet had the same mass, angle of tilt and period of rotation as Earth. The sort of curiosity that attracts curiosity, especially from someone as curious as the Doctor. Alarmed that their crime against Earth was about to be uncovered, the High Council set up an 'inquiry' into the Doctor. The inquiry was held on a secret space station and presided over by an Inquisitor. Initially the Doctor was accused of conduct unbecoming a Time Lord and transgressing the First Law, but ultimately a charge of genocide was brought and the inquiry became a full-scale trial.

The inquiry into the Doctor was held aboard a top-secret space station

The defendant: the Doctor

The prosecutor: the Valeyard

THE INQUISITOR Did none of the unfortunate creatures survive, Doctor?

THE DOCTOR No, my lady. Had even a leaf survived and fallen on fertile soil, a Vervoid would have grown.

THE VALEYARD Every Vervoid was destroyed by your ingenious plan.

THE DOCTOR Yes.

THE VALEYARD Whether or not the Doctor has proved himself innocent of meddling is no longer the cardinal issue before this court. He has proved himself guilty of a far greater crime.

THE INQUISITOR You refer to Article 7 of Gallifreyan law?

THE DOCTOR No, my lady, that cannot apply! Had a single Vervoid reached Earth, the Human race would have been eliminated!

THE VALEYARD Article 7 permits no exceptions. The Doctor has destroyed a complete species. The charge must now be genocide.

Transcript of court proceedings

The Doctor's prosecutor was a Time Lord called the Valeyard. The High Council had made a deal with the Valeyard to adjust the evidence against the Doctor, in return for which he was promised the remainder of the Doctor's regenerations. Extraordinarily, the High Council appear to have done this in full knowledge of who the Valeyard really was: an amalgamation of the darker sides of the Doctor's nature, somewhere between his twelfth and final incarnations.

These revelations led to the collapse of the Doctor's trial. The High Council was deposed and insurrectionists were running amok. With Gallifrey collapsing into chaos, the Master briefly took control of the Matrix. All charges against the Doctor were dropped and he was invited by the Inquisitor to stand for the presidency of a new High Council.

He declined.

CHAPTER FOUR

NOVICES OF
THE UNTEMPERED SCHISM

Before you enter the Capitol for the final time, just a child and already on the threshold of immortality, you are led to an arid patch in the Drylands. There, in the giant shadow of the citadel, sad old men bearing torches usher you inside their circle of flames. You step, stumbling and fearful, across the circular plate, set into the ground and bearing the Seal of Rassilon, to a ring of granite and steel that stands erect and tall, the height of three or four men. And you are faced suddenly with the ultimate impossibility: the Untempered Schism. A gap in the fabric of reality through which you can see the whole of the Vortex. You stand there, 8 years old, staring at the raw power of Time and Space. Will you pass the initiation? Will you be inspired, will you run away, or will you go mad?

The Untempered Schism

When you study the official histories, you get this disconcerting sense of writers tiptoeing daintily around the Problems. It's all lists of dull, grey Presidents: assorted Pundats and Pandaks (I, II, III – now *there* was a President with some staying power; 900 years he lasted), and Greyjan and Saran and Drall, etc., etc., etc. It dodges the difficult ones – not least Morbius and the Doctor – and becomes a sort of encyclopaedia of accepted ideas.

What, then, might a Gallifreyan history look like if it remembered the renegades, the runaways and the run-of-the-mill?

THE ONES THAT WERE INSPIRED

ANDRED Commander in the Chancellery Guard during the Vardan and Sontaran incursions. Led a revolt against the Vardans during which he attempted to assassinate the Doctor, believing that the President was in league with the invaders. Subsequently joined the Doctor's resistance group against the Sontarans. After the invasions were repelled, Andred married Leela of the Sevateem, a former travelling companion of the Doctor, believed to be the first non-Gallifreyan permitted to enter and remain in the Capitol.

ANDRO Technician on duty in the TT Capsule repair shop when the Doctor first stole a TARDIS and fled Gallifrey.

ANDROGAR Liaison between the High Council and Gallifrey High Command at the close of the Last Great Time War.

Andred *Andro* *Androgar*

Damon   _Darkel_   _Engin_

DAMON A Matrix technician during the Second Omega Crisis, he discovered that a member of the High Council had stolen and transmitted the Doctor's biodata extract from the Matrix.

DARKEL The Inquisitor presiding over the trial of the Doctor in his sixth incarnation.

ENGIN Coordinator of the Archives at the time of the assassination of the 406th President.

Fabian

FABIAN Technician on duty in the TT Capsule repair shop when the Doctor first stole a TARDIS and fled Gallifrey.

FLAVIA Chancellor in Borusa's last High Council, she became Acting President when the Doctor responded to his reappointment as President by fleeing Gallifrey. Her presidency was not a great success (see Chapter 3).

THE GENERAL Leader of Gallifrey's High Command in the last days of the Time War, he reluctantly acquiesced in the Doctors' plan to freeze Gallifrey in a single moment in time, leaving

Flavia

The General

the Dalek fleet to obliterate itself. Once Rassilon had succeeded in returning Gallifrey to the universe, hidden at the end of time, the General remained in command of Gallifrey's military. Eventually abandoning Rassilon, the General acknowledged the Doctor as the victor in the Time War, also recognising where his troops' loyalties lay. Having seen Rassilon and the High Council ejected from the planet, the General initially cooperated with the Doctor, until he realised that the Doctor's aim was to extract his companion Clara Oswald from her time stream at the moment of her death. When he refused to help alter the established historical event of Clara's death, the Doctor shot him. This provoked his eleventh regeneration, back into a woman after spending one incarnation in male form.

GOMER Surgeon-General at the time of the Doctor's inauguration as the 407th President, Lord Gomer was expelled from the Capitol on the orders of

Castellan Kelner during the Vardan invasion. There is no record to indicate that he survived the ordeal.

HEDIN A member of the High Council at the time of the Second Omega Crisis. When the Council decided to prevent Omega's return by sacrificing the Doctor, Hedin's was the only dissenting voice. This proved to be a feint to disguise his identity as the traitor on the High Council. He seems to have acted, however, out of a misplaced reverence for the legend of Omega, and he ultimately gave his life to protect the Doctor.

HILRED Commander in the Chancellery Guard at the time of the assassination of the 406th President. He was murdered by the Master.

CASTELLAN JERRICHO The Castellan of the Chancellery Guard, responsible for security on Gallifrey in general and for the President's safety in particular, and member of the High Council during the Second Omega Crisis. Led to believe that the Doctor and President Borusa had conspired to return Omega to Gallifrey, he threatened Borusa and tried to shoot the Doctor, instead killing Hedin, the actual traitor. Still in office when the Death Zone was reactivated, the Castellan was framed by Borusa then murdered by a Chancellery Guard Commander, supposedly while trying to escape.

Gomer

Hedin

Hilred

Castellan Jerricho

Castellan Kelner

Maxil

The Partisan

Rodan

CASTELLAN KELNER The Castellan of the Chancellery Guard, responsible for security on Gallifrey in general and for the President's safety in particular, during the Vardan and Sontaran incursions. When the Doctor relieved Borusa of the presidency, Kelner's loyalties were smoothly transferred, and his allegiance switched just as smartly to the Vardans and then to the Sontarans. He took the opportunity to settle many old scores, locking people up and exiling them from the Capitol. Every oligarchy gets the Castellan it deserves.

MAXIL Commander in the Chancellery Guard at the time of the Second Omega Crisis. He supervised the (abortive) execution of the Doctor.

THE PARTISAN A member of Rassilon's final High Council in the last days of the Time War. She was the first of the Council to suggest that the enormity of the War meant that it was at last time to end it. Rassilon executed her.

RODAN Space Traffic Control technician monitoring activity in the spatial vicinity of Gallifrey before the Vardan and Sontaran incursions. Briefly exiled from the Capitol, she joined the Doctor's resistance group against the Sontarans. Under hypnosis, she assisted in the construction of the De-mat Gun he used to end the invasion.

RUNCIBLE THE FATUOUS Unpopular fellow student of the Doctor and his contemporaries at Prydon Academy, he eventually found his calling as Commentator for the Public Register Video and was on the spot to report on the assassination of the 406th President. Sadly for him, nobody would tell him what had happened; happily for him, the broadcast had already been suspended. He had his moment in court at the Doctor's subsequent trial and was then summoned to help with Castellan Spandrell's inquiries. The Master murdered him with a stake in the back.

SAVAR A contemporary and colleague of the Lord Gomer, but lacking his interest in wavelength broadcast power transduction.

CASTELLAN SPANDRELL The Castellan of the Chancellery Guard, responsible for security on Gallifrey in general and for the President's safety in particular, at the time of the assassination of the 406th President. Denied the chance to investigate that murder before the trial of the accused, he came to accept the Doctor's protestations of innocence and helped him expose Chancellor Goth and the Master's plot.

TALOR Colleague of Matrix technician Damon, he was murdered by Councillor Hedin.

Runcible the Fatuous

Savar

Castellan Spandrell

Talor

Thalia · The Woman · Zorac

THALIA Chancellor in Borusa's first High Council during the Second Omega Crisis, she voted with her peers to execute the Doctor. It is rumoured that she was among the High Council members despatched into the Death Zone by Borus, ostensibly to investigate what was going on there. If so, she did not survive.

THE WOMAN One of only two members of Rassilon's final High Council in the last days of the Time War to vote against the Lord President's plan to return Gallifrey to the universe. Her punishment was to stand as a monument to her own shame 'like the Weeping Angels of old', and her name was erased from time.

ZORAC Cardinal in Borusa's first High Council during the Second Omega Crisis, he voted with his peers to execute the Doctor. It is rumoured that he was among the High Council members despatched into the Death Zone by Borusa, ostensibly to investigate what was going on there. If so, he did not survive.

THE ONES THAT WENT MAD

BORUSA Formerly a tutor at Prydon Academy, his erstwhile pupils included the Doctor, the Master, the Rani and Drax. He specialised in mathematics, reason and mental powers. Elevated to the High Council as a Cardinal shortly before the assassination of the 406th President, Borusa oversaw the

Borusa

repairs and renovations to the Capitol after the Master's attempt to open the Eye of Harmony. The Council subsequently ratified Borusa's appointment as Chancellor and he thus became Acting President until the Doctor's return to Gallifrey. He played a vital role in the defeat of the Vardans and Sontarans.

Following the Doctor's resignation, Borusa legitimately became President, in which capacity he later sanctioned the Doctor's execution in an effort to prevent the return of Omega to this universe. Possibly caused by his

Borusa

Goth

involvement in several major crises in quick succession, Borusa underwent three regenerations in a very short space of time. These culminated in an incarnation that believed he had earned the right to rule Gallifrey in perpetuity, having governed the Time Lords, openly and behind the scenes, for so long. Borusa had located the Black Scrolls of Rassilon and followed the clues that would lead him to immortality. Rassilon duly rewarded him with a living death in the Dark Tower. The legends say that Borusa was later resurrected to help the Time Lords through dark periods of rebellion and war, even somehow serving Rassilon during the Time War.

GOTH Prydonian Chancellor at the time of the assassination of the 406th President, whom he was generally expected to succeed – and eventually revealed as the assassin. He encountered the dying Master on Tersurus and agreed to transport him to Gallifrey. There, he claimed, he found himself unable to resist the Master's mental control and colluded in the scheme to kill the President and frame the Doctor. The Master used him to enter and manipulate the Matrix, and to ensure that the Doctor would be promptly executed for the assassination. Goth ultimately perished when the Master left him trapped in the Matrix and he was killed by the psychosomatic feedback.

THE MASTER THE OFFICIAL RECORD: There is no official record of any Time Lord ever adopting that title, and no biodata extract exists for him.

THE MASTER THE UNOFFICIAL RECORD: Bad. Evil, cunning and resourceful. Highly developed powers of extrasensory perception and a formidable hypnotist. Brilliant at mathematics. A stupendous egotist. And, more than any other Time Lord, the creation of Rassilon.

He was a contemporary of the Doctor's and a fellow student at Prydon Academy. At the moment of his initiation at the Untempered Schism, he heard a rhythm, a torment that stayed with him for the rest of his life. This sound of drums was implanted in his mind by Rassilon – four beats transmitted back through time. Rassilon's intention was to create a link from the very end of the Time War through which he could restore Gallifrey. That it drove the Master insane was immaterial. He heard the sound of drums through all his lives and became Gallifrey's most infamous child.

In his earliest years, all he did was cause trouble, but the Master's ambitions grew quickly. At the time of the Doctor's banishment to Earth, the Master made the conquest or destruction of that world his pet project. He opened the way for the Nestene Consciousness to make its second attack on the planet. He brought an alien mind parasite to Earth and attempted to provoke a third world war. He colluded with Axos, tried to control a Dæmon and revived a colony of marine reptiles that had ruled Earth millions of years earlier. He hoped to

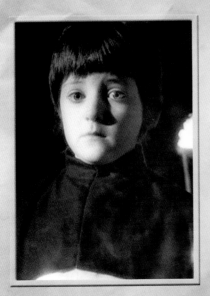 

The Master

The Master

blackmail the galaxy with the Uxariean Doomsday Weapon or see it decimated by the Daleks. He even roused a Chronovore.

An existence even more rackety than the Doctor's took its toll, and the Master reached the end of his thirteenth life while the Doctor was still in his fourth. His attempt to regenerate himself using the Eye of Harmony was foiled (see Chapter 3), but he later succeeded in harnessing the power of the Keepership of the Traken Union to enable him to take over a Trakenite body. In this unnaturally prolonged form, the Master came close to bringing the universe to a premature end: utterly misunderstanding the role of Logopolis in maintaining the causal nexus, he brought that world to a complete halt. As the collapse of the universe accelerated, the Master and the Doctor formed a very temporary alliance; the universe (or most of it) was saved, at the cost of the Doctor's fourth life.

Failing to trap the newly regenerated Doctor in a recursive occlusion, the Master was successively stranded in the prehistories of the planets Earth and Xeriphas. On Xeriphas, he discovered a prototype android shape-shifter dubbed Kamelion, which was instrumental in his escape. Exerting a mental hold over the android, he planned to use it to disrupt history, but a test run on thirteenth-century Earth was halted by the Doctor. The Master's mental link with Kamelion was later severed and the android was destroyed.

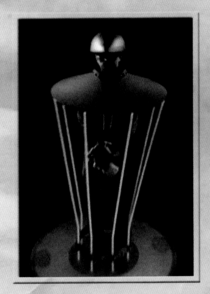

The Master

Around this time, the Master received an unexpected summons from Gallifrey. The Death Zone had been reactivated and the Doctor – in all his regenerations – had vanished from space and time (see Chapter 3). In desperation, the Inner Council overruled President Borusa and asked for the Master's help in rescuing the Doctor. His reward would be a complete new cycle of regenerations, a pledge they avoided having to honour.

When the Doctor, in his sixth incarnation, was put on trial, the Master intervened in the closing stages of the hearing. He revealed the true identity of the Valeyard and the true origin of the planet Ravalox, hoping to take control of the Time Lords in the resulting chaos. When the extent of the High Council's corruption was exposed, there was rioting and insurrection on Gallifrey, and the Master became trapped inside the Matrix. He escaped or was set free.

By this stage, the Master's stolen Trakenite body was nearing its end. After a near-fatal encounter with a semi-feline species, however, he discovered some new way to transfer his consciousness from one form to another. In this way, he survived execution by the Daleks. He took over a male Human and set a trap for the eighth Doctor, intending to relieve him of his remaining regenerations, once again by tapping the power of the Eye of Harmony. His attempt failed, and he was sucked into the Eye.

The Master

There are many rumours and stories of what happened to the Master next: some say that he was saved from inside the Vortex by the mythical Esterath; some say that he remained trapped in the Doctor's TARDIS, his mental resources transferred into an android, acting as the Doctor's companion or pet. Others say simply that he was, finally, dead.

Dead, until the advent of the Time War, that is. It is certain that the Time Lords resurrected him as a perfect warrior for the War: his past sins forgotten, if not forgiven, the Master was given a new regeneration cycle and fought alongside his people against the Daleks. Then came the fall of the Cruciform to the Dalek Emperor, and the Master fled to the Silver Devastation, 100 trillion years into the future. He used a Chameleon Arch to make himself a Human child, hoping never to be found. The infant grew up to become a professor named Yana, the last hope of the last Humans as the universe neared its end. And that's where he was – still plagued by the sound of drums – when the Doctor arrived, inadvertently causing Professor Yana to realise his true identity and shed his humanity.

Another regeneration followed, and the Master seized control of twenty-first-century Earth, turning the planet into a giant weapons factory that would wage war on the universe. Defeated again by the Doctor, the Master chose

The Master or Missy

death, for the first time in all his lives. Perhaps the Doctor should have been suspicious; perhaps he was, and that's why he burnt the Master's corpse. But the Master, as always, cheated death – his consciousness now held within a ring. His followers retrieved the ring and brought him back to life. The process was only partially successful, though, and the renewed Master found that he was burning up energy more quickly than he could feed. By now utterly deranged, he transplanted his mind into every Human on planet Earth. That was the moment that Rassilon's plans reached fruition, and Gallifrey re-emerged into the universe via its link with the Master (see Chapter 6). As the Doctor severed that link, the Master turned on Rassilon.

Though Rassilon's plan failed on that occasion, the ultimate return of Gallifrey to reality was, of course, assured (see Chapter 7). And with it came the Master, now regenerated into female form and calling herself Missy. Missy created an army of Cybermen out of the dead on twenty-first-century Earth, then travelled to Skaro with the Doctor, where she was last seen surrounded by Daleks.

THE MONK An inveterate time meddler, the Monk stole a Mark IV Type 40 capsule and left Gallifrey some fifty years after the Doctor. Like the Doctor, he was attracted to the planet Earth, but his primary motivations were apparently fun and profit. Having introduced Leonardo da Vinci to the idea of powered flight, he decided to change a key point in Earth history, planning to destroy an eleventh-century Viking fleet so that the Saxon King Harold would defeat the Norman William at the Battle of Hastings. Anticipating that this change would avert a series of wars in the continent of Europe, he claimed he wanted to bring peace and allow Earth's Humans to better themselves. With a few hints and tips from him, he thought, Humanity might develop jet airliners by 1320; Shakespeare could see his plays performed on television…

Outwitted by the Doctor, the Monk was stranded in eleventh-century Northumbria but eventually escaped to the planet Tigus and then to Earth's ancient Egypt. There he entered a succession of uneasy alliances with the Doctor and with the Daleks, eventually being stranded again on an unidentified ice planet.

MORBIUS A war criminal who once led the High Council of the Time Lords. A ruthless dictator, but with millions of fanatical followers and admirers. He took a mercenary army to Karn, promising them immortality. When Morbius and his rebels overran the planet, the Time Lords saved the Sisterhood. Morbius was executed on Karn: his body was placed in a dispersal chamber

The Monk

Morbius

and atomised, but his brain was secretly preserved by one of his Human
followers. Dr Mehendri Solon was one of the foremost neurosurgeons of his
time, an expert in microsurgical tissue-transplant techniques. Solon spent
several years constructing a new physical form for Morbius by scavenging body
parts from crashed spacecraft crews. When Solon activated the monstrosity
he had created, the Doctor challenged Morbius to a mind-bending contest –
it nearly killed the Doctor but was enough to overheat Morbius's brain. The
Sisterhood then forced him off a mountain side, and he fell, presumably, to
his final death. (There are, as always, terrible stories that Morbius somehow
managed to escape death again.)

THE RANI A contemporary of the Doctor's and a fellow student at Prydon
Academy, the Rani was a scientific genius, but obsessive to the point of madness.
She was expelled from Gallifrey after her experiments on mice created monsters
that ate the President's cat and took a chunk out of the President too. She
enslaved the world of Miasimia Goria, whose inhabitants she relieved of the
chemicals in the brain that they needed to sleep; this drove her subjects violently

The Rani   *Salyavin*

insane. She continued her experiments on nineteenth-century Earth until stopped by the Doctor. Taking control of the planet Lakertya, she began stealing geniuses from their time streams in order to build a time manipulator. The final mind she needed was the Doctor's, and she caused his sixth regeneration when she trapped his TARDIS. He returned the favour, trapping her in her own TARDIS with a bunch of Tetraps.

SALYAVIN A great criminal, with a unique talent: the capacity to project his mind into other minds. He was imprisoned in the Time Prison on Shada but escaped, using his mental abilities to force the Time Lords to forget not only him but also Shada itself. Stealing *The Ancient and Worshipful Law of Gallifrey* from the Panopticon Archives to ensure that his escape remained undetected, he assumed a new identity and went into hiding. Now calling himself Chronotis, he became a Professor at the University of Cambridge on seventeenth-century Earth, staying there for 300 years until he was located by the Dronoid criminal Skagra. There is a theory that temporal instabilities have caused this chain of events to unfold on at least four occasions, involving at least two different incarnations of the Doctor.

THE VISIONARY Tattooed affiliate of Rassilon's final High Council in the last days of the Time War. Her ceaseless predictions suggested that only two Time Lords, the Doctor and the Master, would survive the War. She also gave Rassilon the idea of implanting a link with Gallifrey in the Master's mind in order to restore the planet.

THE WAR CHIEF A near-contemporary of the Doctor's at the Academy, he also stole a TARDIS and left Gallifrey. He gave time-travel technology to an alien species from Galactic Sector 973, helping them mastermind 'war games' intended to breed an ultimate fighting force with the aim of bringing about a United Galactic Empire – preferably with himself as Supreme Galactic Ruler. The Doctor's intervention halted the games, and the War Chief was executed by his alien collaborators. There is a record of the aliens' War Lord being put on trial by the Time Lords; the sentence was that the War Lord, his entire species and his home world would all be dematerialised, so that they would never have existed. No trace of them remains, not even their name.

The Visionary

The War Chief

THE ONES THAT RAN AWAY

ABLIF Member of the Outsiders, a group of former Time Lords who had chosen to leave the Capitol and generally get back to nature. He joined the resistance effort against the Vardans and the Sontarans and was killed by a Sontaran.

AZMAEL Formerly a tutor at Prydon Academy, his erstwhile pupils included the Doctor, the Master, the Rani and Drax. With that pedigree, it's little surprise that he also renounced Time Lord society. Absconding from Gallifrey, he became Master of the planet Jaconda. He died saving the Jacondan people from Mestor, a giant Gastropod.

THE CORSAIR An adventurer in time and space, who lost his life to House, an entity that fed on Artron energy and had trapped and killed countless Time Lords and TARDISes.

THE DOCTOR Disappointing graduate of the Prydonian Academy, achieving only 51 per cent at his second attempt, he never amounted to anything in the galaxy owing to his propensity for vulgar facetiousness.

DRAX Undistinguished contemporary of the Doctor's at Prydon Academy, who failed Temporal Theory. He left Gallifrey and travelled the galaxy. He made use of his practical skills to provide technical repair and maintenance services in cybernetics, guidance systems and armaments; he also bought up defunct technology, repaired it and sold it on at a profit. After a 'hyperbolics failure' in

Ablif

Azmael

Drax

The Doctor

K'anpo Rimpoche   *Nesbin*   *Presta*

his TARDIS systems, he was stranded on Earth for a time, and served a ten-year prison sentence in Brixton, London. He eventually ended up on Zeos, a world in the Helical galaxy then in the final stages of a prolonged nuclear war with its twin planet, Atrios. There he worked for the Shadow, an agent of the Guardian of Darkness and Chaos, installing a battle computer called Mentalis to fight the war.

K'ANPO RIMPOCHE At one time a respected teacher at the Academy, he elected to leave Time Lord society but remain on Gallifrey. Leaving the Capitol, he became a hermit, sitting under a tree halfway up a mountain, giving nature lessons to the local children, among them the Doctor. He awakened the Doctor's curiosity about and love of life in all its forms, and also told him tales of the giant vampires fought by Rassilon. Leaving Gallifrey, he journeyed to Earth, becoming Abbot of a monastery where the Doctor, at the end of his third life, again met him and followed his spiritual guidance.

NESBIN Leader of the Outsiders, a group of former Time Lords who had chosen to leave the Capitol and generally get back to nature. He joined the resistance effort against the Vardans and the Sontarans.

PRESTA Member of the Outsiders, a group of former Time Lords who had chosen to leave the Capitol and generally get back to nature. She joined the resistance effort against the Vardans and the Sontarans.

ROMANADVORATRELUNDAR The Lady Romanadvoratrelundar graduated from the Academy with a triple first, specialising in History and

Romanadvoratrelundar

Psychology. Aged 139, she was working in the Bureau of Ancient Records when she was selected by the Guardian of Light and Time to assist the Doctor in his quest for the six segments of the Key to Time. Together, they travelled to Ribos, Zanak, Earth, Tara, the third moon of Delta Magna, and the twin planets Atrios and Zeos in the Helical galaxy. Romana (her name was shortened by the Doctor) was a good student of the Academy – precise, logical, practical, everything by the book. Having never previously ventured outside the Capitol, she was totally inexperienced, but learned rapidly from her experiences.

Their mission completed, Romana was expecting to return to Gallifrey, but decided to stay with the Doctor. She also chose to initiate a controlled regeneration, selecting the form of a princess of Atrios as her template. Her second incarnation, sharper and wittier than her first, demonstrated quite how much she'd picked up from the Doctor; she even started lying about her age. They stopped the Daleks retrieving Davros from Skaro, saved prehistoric Earth from destruction by the last of the Jagaroth, freed a Tythonian ambassador from imprisonment on the planet Chloris, halted illegal trafficking in the drug Vraxoin, and ended the Nimon's 'great journey of life'. She was involved in the events surrounding Salyavin's imprisonment on Shada on at least two occasions with at least two different incarnations of the Doctor.

Romana and the Doctor also prevented a renewed conflict between the Argolin and the Foamasi, and stopped the last Zolfa-Thuran, Meglos, reactivating the Screens of Zolfa-Thura. At this point, the Time Lords summoned her home to Gallifrey, but she refused to go back. The Doctor's TARDIS then travelled through a Charged Vacuum Emboitment and was lost in E-Space for a time. When it re-emerged into our N-Space, the last of the great vampires (see Chapter 1) had been slain, but Romana was no longer aboard. She had elected to remain at the gateway into E-Space to help with the liberation of an enslaved time-sensitive race, the Tharils.

Eventually, Romana returned to this universe and to Gallifrey, where she replaced Flavia as President in the wake of the insurrections that followed the exposure of the Ravalox affair. Her abduction by the Daleks during the Etra Prime incident was an early warning of the Time War to come (see Chapters 3 and 5).

'SUSAN' One of the Time Lords' many great and undiscussed mysteries. When the Doctor first left Gallifrey, he took with him a child, a daughter of the President. He called her Susan; she called him Grandfather. Some say that she devised the acronym TARDIS for our time-travel capsules. Records of her true identity and history seem to have been deliberately obscured, and we are left with competing mythologies. She may have been a direct descendant of Rassilon or of some other founding father of Gallifrey.
Her original name may have been Larn, or it may have been Arkytior. She undoubtedly travelled with the Doctor for some time, and is known to have visited Akhaten, Quinnis, Skaro, Marinus and the Sense-Sphere, as well as Earth during its prehistory and in its thirteenth, fifteenth and eighteenth centuries. She appears to have settled in London for several months in the 1960s and again in the late twenty-second century, where she is believed to have married a Human named Campbell or Cameron. Oddly, and perhaps because official knowledge of her is so hazy, the Doctor's Malfeasance Tribunal made no attempt to establish her fate.

'Susan'

CHAPTER FIVE

GALLIFREY FALLS...

When the Time Lords sent the Doctor to Skaro to avert the genesis of the Daleks, they inadvertently began a conflict that wrought havoc throughout history, in all times and all places...

When the Daleks attempted to assassinate the High Council on Gallifrey using duplicates of the Doctor and his associates, they inadvertently began a conflict that wrought havoc throughout history, in all times and all places...

When the Daleks abducted President Romanadvoratrelundar from Etra Prime, they inadvertently began a conflict that wrought havoc throughout history, in all times and all places...

When the self-declared President-Elect of the High Council of Time Lords, Keeper of the Legacy of Rassilon, Defender of the Laws of Time, Protector of Gallifrey, used the Hand of Omega to destroy Skaro, he inadvertently began a conflict that wrought havoc throughout history, in all times and all places...

When the Master survived his execution by the Daleks, thus breaking the peace treaty opened by President Romana under the Act of Master Restitution, he inadvertently began a conflict that wrought havoc throughout history, in all times and all places...

The destruction of Skaro (above) and the ensuing conflict between the Daleks and Time Lords (overleaf)

Davros, creator of the Daleks

How do you tell the history of a war when nobody is really sure how it even started? How do you tell the history of a war in which every action has happened, then not happened at all, then happened again but at a different time entirely? A war that neither side has survived, yet both sides have survived. The Time War erupted through every time and no time and left the universe in an infinite state of temporal flux, and only one man truly knew how it ended. And even he was mostly wrong.

What do we know (or think we know)? The Daleks vanished from time and space after the Tenth Dalek Occupation. Galactic folklore said that they had gone off to fight a bigger war. The Dalek Emperor led his entire race into the Vortex and let loose the Deathsmiths of Goth. The Time Lords simultaneously deployed a fleet of Bowships, Black Hole Carriers and N-Forms time-scooped from their ancient history. In the first year of the War, Davros was killed when his command ship flew into the jaws of the Nightmare Child at the Gates of Elysium. The Doctor witnessed his death and may even have tried to prevent it.

The Time War raged and shook the universe. The Sontarans were turned away from what they regarded as the finest war in history; other Lesser Species remained oblivious to the changes and un-changes being visited upon their histories. Higher Species like the Forest of Cheem watched and despaired, and some were directly affected. The Gelth lost their physical forms and were marooned in a gaseous half-life; it turned them into killers. The Greater Animus and its Carsenome were destroyed. The Eternals finally forsook this reality.

The Daleks became able to absorb the background radiation generated by time travel and use it as a power supply. By the end of the conflict, the Daleks' ideals of genetic purity and uniformity had been weakened, and the Emperor had created a secret order, the Cult of Skaro, giving it complete autonomy. Before the War's end, the Cult had escaped into the Void between parallel dimensions with a stolen Time Lord prison ship containing millions of Daleks. There they waited,

Gallifrey's augmented troopers

developing theories for how to evolve new, stronger forms of Dalek.

The Time Lords, meanwhile, resurrected the Master – the perfect warrior in a Time War. But when the Dalek Emperor took control of the Cruciform, the Master ran as far as he could go, to the farthest reaches of space 100 trillion years into the future, and disguised himself as a Human child.

Every forbidden weapon was taken from the Omega Arsenal in the Time Vaults down in the depths of Gallifrey. Soldiers were re-engineered, time-sensitive surveillance equipment and weaponry grafted onto them, installing hard drives into their brains. The bio-engineered troopers began reporting premonitions – of their own deaths, of the fall of their race – but High Command dismissed these as hallucinations.

The Time Lords now showed total disregard for the effects of their actions on weaker species. Entire planets and whole civilisations were sacrificed. Millions of lesser races were dying with every second that passed, only for Time itself to resurrect them, only to find new ways of dying, again and again and again. Unimaginable horrors, new and ancient, were born and reborn in the conflict: the Skaro Degradations, the Horde of Travesties, the Couldhavebeen King, the Army of Meanwhiles and Neverweres...

The Time War turned into Hell.

At some stage in the conflict, the Time Lords turned to their founding father: Rassilon himself was resurrected. Leaving the conduct of the War to the

generals in High Command, Rassilon retreated with his High Council to a protected void, linked to the Capitol, but in a separate dimension. There he developed a devastating Final Sanction: a plan to rupture the Time Vortex and destroy all life in the universe, while the Time Lords would ascend to become creatures of consciousness alone. In this non-corporeal form, they would be unaffected by time or cause and effect, while the rest of the cosmos was destroyed.

Through most of this, the Doctor had stood aside from the Time War. He refused to fight and intervened only to help the victims. He tried to save the Nestene home world but had to watch as the Consciousness lost its protein planets and all its food stocks. Ultimately, he lost his eighth life trying to save the lone Human survivor of a gunship, which crash-landed on Karn with him aboard. There, the Doctor was restored to life by the Sisterhood. Their leader Ohila confronted the Doctor, condemning his refusal to join the War. She

Rassilon the Resurrected

132

The Nestene Consciousness

'Physician, heal thyself.'

told him that all reality was threatened and blamed him for the continuing deaths – he, she said, was the universe's last hope. Finally persuaded, he accepted a potion that would regenerate him into a warrior.

For decades, this War Doctor led Time Lords in battle against the Daleks and fought on the front line, from the Tantalus Eye to Skull Moon. The soldiers of Gallifrey had a saying:

'The first thing you will notice about the Doctor of War is he's unarmed. For many, it's also the last.' Then, finally, the War Doctor came to Arcadia.

Gallifrey itself had remained at the furthest edge of the War, but it became the setting for its end when the Daleks managed to breach the previously impenetrable Sky Trenches protecting Gallifrey's

The Daleks penetrate the Sky Trenches

The Daleks attack Arcadia

second city. The final Dalek assault transformed the surface of Gallifrey. The valley between the mountains of Solace and Solitude was a pit of fire, and the shattered hulls of downed Dalek spaceships were strewn across the burning landscape. The glass dome surrounding the Capitol was cracked, left open to the elements and, in the ancient edifices beneath, broken roofs and ancient stone and metal were aflame.

In the skies above, every Dalek ship in the cosmos had converged on Gallifrey. The planet was surrounded, endless Dalek firepower raining down. The Sky Trenches above the Capitol were holding, but it was only a matter of time before they, too, would be breached. This was the last day of the Last Great Time War.

Dalek saucers converge on Gallifrey

The War Doctor witnessed Arcadia's fall and made a vow: No More. With the entire War time-locked, so neither side could escape and no other beings could enter it, the Doctor breached the Omega Arsenal, deep below the Capitol. He removed the one last weapon that no Time Lord had yet dared to deploy, the final work of the ancients of Gallifrey: a weapon so powerful, its operating system had become sentient and developed a conscience. A weapon of ultimate mass destruction that could eat a galaxy, but not until it had stood in judgement over its user. The Moment.

When Rassilon the Resurrected learned that the Doctor had taken the Moment, he realised that it meant the end for Daleks and Gallifreyans alike.

The Moment

The Visionary, who now sat on the High Council, had prophesied that just two Time Lords would survive: the Doctor and the Master. Desperate to avert the impending destruction of his world, his race and its billion-year history, Rassilon devised a way to implant a psychic link between Gallifrey and the Master's mind. The link's point of physical contact was a diamond, a Whitepoint Star, which Rassilon sent to twenty-first-century Earth.

Rassilon's Inner Council

RASSILON What news of the Doctor?

CHANCELLOR Disappeared, my Lord President.

DARTISAN But we know his intention. He still possesses the Moment. And he'll use it, to destroy Daleks and Time Lords alike.

CHANCELLOR The Visionary confirms it...

VISIONARY ... ending, burning, falling, all of it falling, the black and pitch and screaming fire, so burning...

CHANCELLOR All of her prophecies say the same. That this is the last day of the Time War. That Gallifrey falls; that we die, today.

VISIONARY ... ending ending *ending ENDING!*

DARTISAN Perhaps it's time. This is only the furthest edge of the Time War. But at its heart, millions die every second. Lost in bloodlust and insanity. With Time itself resurrecting them, to find new ways of dying, over and over again. A travesty of life. Isn't it better to end it? At last?

RASSILON Thank you for your opinion. I will not die. Do you hear me? A billion years of Time Lord history riding on our backs, I will not let this perish, I will *not*!

CHANCELLOR ... There is, um... there is one part of the prophecy, my Lord. Forgive me, I'm sorry, it's rather difficult to decipher, but... It talks of two survivors, beyond the Final Day. Two children of Gallifrey.

RASSILON Does it name them? ☞

CHANCELLOR It foresees them locked in their final confrontation. The Enmity of Ages. Which would suggest…

RASSILON The Doctor. And the Master.

CHANCELLOR One word keeps being repeated, my Lord. One constant word. Earth.

VISIONARY … earth earth earth earth earth earth…

CHANCELLOR Planet Earth. Indigenous species: the Human race.

VISIONARY … earth earth earth…

RASSILON Maybe that's where the answer lies. Our salvation. On Earth…

Session of the Inner Council

On Gallifrey, the War Doctor, in possession of the Moment, now had the means to end the Time War completely. Today was the day it wasn't possible to do the right thing. He trudged alone across the Drylands, to a place he'd once called home. He thought of everything he had seen, all the suffering. He thought how every instant in Time and Space was burning. It must end, he decided, and he meant to end it the only way he could. The Moment of decision. He thought of Gallifrey's children, and wondered how many of them he would be killing that day. He vowed that, one terrible day, he would count them. And then he activated the Moment.

Both great battle fleets, tens of millions of ships, and both home worlds were obliterated. The Daleks and the Time Lords died burning and screaming in an inferno that lasted just a single second. The Doctor saw Gallifrey and Skaro reduced to rocks and dust, and walked away from the ruins entirely alone – the only survivor of the Last Great Time War.

CHAPTER SIX

... NO MORE

The man who walked away
from that devastation had
forsaken the name of the
Doctor. As he regenerated,
he resolved to earn the name back
again, shutting away all memory of the
warrior he had been, never admitting
– even to himself – that a War Doctor
had ever existed. A new Doctor was
born: a man who made people better;
a man determined to make reparation;
a man who survived the guilt only by
telling himself that it had somehow
been worth it. *

But the Daleks survived. They always
survived, while he lost everything.

First he discovered a lone Dalek
survivor, then an entire new race of
Daleks forged from Human remains
by the Emperor of the Daleks. The
Emperor had survived somehow, his

The War Doctor

---

* The numbering gets tricky here. Let's call this one the ninth.

The Emperor of the Daleks

The Genesis Ark

ship falling through time, crippled but alive. But the Doctor sang a song, and the Daleks ran away.

And, always, they came back. The Cult of Skaro, hidden in the Void, burst back into the universe, opening their stolen Time Lord prison ship – their Genesis Ark – to unleash millions of Daleks across planet Earth. The tenth Doctor sent them back into Hell, but the Cult of Skaro escaped… The Doctor saw the Cult destroyed, but one escaped… The Doctor had seen Davros perish in the jaws of the Nightmare Child, but then came Davros with yet more Daleks, carved from the flesh of his own body…

There had been a flicker of hope that he was not alone. The Visionary had been right: two survivors, two children of Gallifrey – the Doctor and the Master. A Master now driven so completely insane by the sound of drums that he no longer had the

The Master – driven insane by the sound of drums

patience to delay an execution to pull the wings off a fly. The Master decimated the Human race, just for fun, and then won a final victory over the Doctor by choosing to die. Not that the Master ever really dies, of course. Back he came, madder than ever, taking control of Earth once again and transplanting himself into every Human being on the planet. And then the Master found a Whitepoint Star…

The entire world of Gallifrey was able to follow the link, out of the time-locked Time War, to Earth. Gallifrey would actually replace the planet Earth in space. Knowing that the Time Lords were returning, the Doctor was forced to confront the truth of why he had used the Moment: that the Time War had changed the Time Lords to the core; that the Time Lords were more dangerous than anything. When Rassilon declared that he would initiate his Final Sanction, the Doctor faced the moment of decision, again.

He made the same choice, shattering the Whitepoint Star, breaking the link, sending Rassilon and the Time Lords back into the Time War.

Back into Hell.

Time moves in mysterious ways. Just before he faced the Master and Rassilon, this Doctor had been having fun, travelling about, getting into trouble. He saw the Phosphorous Carousel of the Great Magellan Gestadt, saved a planet from the Red Carnivorous Maw, named a galaxy Alison, and married Elizabeth I, Queen of England on Earth. And then completely forgot that he had only just been part of the true – entirely different – resolution of the Time War. Only the members of the War Council on the last day of the Time War ever knew how Gallifrey survived. And they never really understood it.

Three versions of the Doctor – the eleventh, the tenth, the warrior – in the same place at the same time. Well, there are precedents: times of wild catastrophes and sudden calls to man the battle stations. The last day of the Last Great Time War must have been the wildest catastrophe of them all.

Three versions of the Doctor, gathered in that barn in the Drylands that he had once called home. Their hands hovered over the Moment, each resolved to share the responsibility and the guilt of what they were about to do.

And then they changed their minds.

An impossible message was transmitted to Gallifrey High Command:

GALLIFREY STANDS

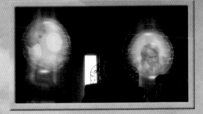
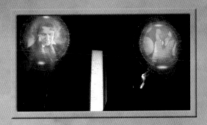
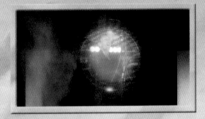

Three versions of the Doctor flew their TARDISes to equidistant points in the planet's lower atmosphere, with an incredible plan to freeze the whole of Gallifrey in a single moment of time, held in a parallel pocket universe. In an instant, Gallifrey would seem simply to blink out of existence, leaving the combined firepower of every Dalek in creation trained on every other Dalek in creation.

The Daleks were wiped out – give or take. And, to anyone watching, it seemed that Gallifrey, too, was gone. The universe stood up, shook itself down, and got on with life, and Time Lords and Daleks became the stuff of myths and folk tales.

The calculations to pull this off would have taken centuries, of course – a dozen lifetimes, perhaps. Lord Androgar, that half-mad relic of the War Council, claims that there were not just three Doctors present on that day. He insists that nine other Doctors announced themselves to the War Council, and that a thirteenth turned up as well.

When I asked the General, she refused to confirm a word of it.

Gallifrey Falls No More

In the Under Gallery of the National Gallery in London on the planet Earth, there is an extraordinary painting. It might be called *No More*, or it might be called *Gallifrey Falls*. The image within it seems to shift, to embody more dimensions than can be possible. It depicts the savage bombardment of a great citadel on an alien world. The night sky is a burned orange and, wherever any part of it catches the light, it looks like a world on fire.

It looks for all the worlds as if the artist has, somehow, captured and frozen a single moment, a slice of real time.

CHAPTER SEVEN

GALLIFREY RISES

Gallifrey was saved. It was no better off, but at least it was saved.

Rassilon now faced several immediate problems. Restoring Gallifrey to the universe was simple enough in principle: the planet was preserved in the equivalent of a gigantic stasis cube; it was therefore as straightforward a process to exit it as it would be to walk free from a painting. The larger question was when and where to do it.

The Matrix had already registered a split in the skin of reality, a time field manifesting as cracks throughout time

A split in the skin of reality

Trenzalore: the most dangerous place in space and time

and space – weak points in the fabric of the universe. Assuming it was the right universe, that was the way out, but where and when would be safe? Emerge at the wrong point, and the Time War would simply erupt anew, a war that would never end. So Rassilon decided to transmit a message through one of the cracks to the Doctor, a question that only the Doctor could answer. If the Doctor heard and spoke his true name, Rassilon would know it was safe for Gallifrey to come through.

Time Lords have always been good at doing things on a cosmic scale. The message was sent out through a crack on the tiny, insignificant world of Trenzalore, and it rang out through all of space and time to all the dark corners of creation. It was said that every sentient being in the universe who detected that signal felt an overpowering sense of fear. Despite this, they all went to Trenzalore – Cybermen, Judoon, Sontarans, *Homo reptilia*, Raxacoricofallapatorians, Terileptils, Sycorax, Weeping Angels… and Daleks. Rassilon had been trying to find the safest place in space and time for Gallifrey's return; instead, he had created the most dangerous.

The Church of the Papal Mainframe cordoned off Trenzalore, maintaining an uneasy truce by blocking every species

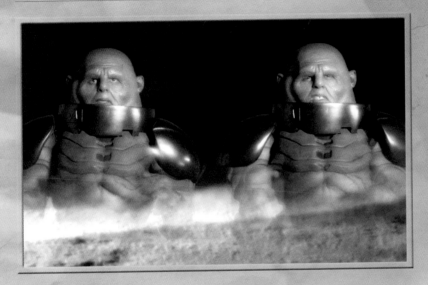

Trenzalore was attacked by Sontarans...

... Cybermen...　　　　　　　*... and Daleks*

Trenzalore, defended by the Church of the Papal Mainframe…

from accessing the planet. The Doctor was sent down to investigate and, being the Doctor, ended up defending a whole world. For centuries, he protected Trenzalore until every attacking race bar the Daleks had either retreated or been destroyed. Eventually, the Daleks would attack in force.

… and the Doctor, to the end of his lives

By the time they did, the Doctor was nearing the end of his lives, all his regenerations used up, and he had no way to stop the Daleks. His Human travelling companion, Clara Oswald, appealed – through the crack – to the Time Lords to help the Doctor. The High Council heard her words, and Rassilon acted. The Doctor was granted a new regeneration cycle. As the time field closed, the Doctor's regeneration energy obliterated the entire Dalek force.

At least Rassilon had found the right universe. He evidently decided on a quieter, less well-announced return, slipping Gallifrey back to its original spatial coordinates, but at the very end of the time continuum, hidden away, safe at the end of the universe. So far into the

The Sisterhood of Karn return to Rassilon's world

future, there was nothing to threaten the Time Lords, no other life but immortals. Immortals, Rassilon realised with some irritation, including the Sisterhood of Karn.

Now Gallifrey could be rebuilt. Mighty towers sprang up around the citadels, row upon row of them, spreading across the Drylands. It was time to make new advances, create new technologies, build new weapons.

It was also time to face the next problem. The Visionary had been so certain, so insistent, on that final day of the Time War, that Gallifrey would fall, that only two Time Lords – the Doctor and the Master – would survive. True, the Doctor and the Master – Missy – were still out there. Yet Gallifrey stood and the Time Lords endured. Rassilon's thoughts turned to the ancient legends of the Hybrid, the unstoppable creature that would bring about the end of the Time Lords, the end of Gallifrey, the end of Time (see Chapter 1). It would be crossbred from two great warrior species, forced together to create a warrior greater than either – that much was known. So it had to be the Daleks and the Time Lords, that would make sense.

Rassilon believed that the Doctor had information about the Hybrid. Why

A new Gallifrey rises

did he think that? Perhaps somebody had been whispering in his ear, after she escaped from the Daleks on Skaro. For whatever reason, Rassilon was convinced, and determined to extract the information. He gave the order for Clara Oswald to be killed and the Doctor trapped and imprisoned inside his own Confession Dial, not to be released until he admitted what he knew of the Hybrid.

Eventually, after an imprisonment of four and a half billion years, the Doctor did confess that he knew something:

Long before the Time War, the Time Lords knew it was coming, like a storm on the wind. There were many prophecies and stories, legends before the fact. One of them was about a creature called the Hybrid. Half-Dalek, half-Time Lord, the ultimate warrior. But whose side would it be on? Would it bring peace or destruction? Was it real, or a fantasy? I confess, I know the Hybrid is real. I know where it is, and what it is. I confess, I'm afraid.

Extract from the Doctor's
Confession Dial

The Doctor broke free from his prison, and stepped onto the surface of Gallifrey for the first time since the last day of the Time War. As he began to walk across the Drylands, he came across a young Gallifreyan, just 7 years old. And he spoke to me:

Go to the city. Find somebody important. Tell them I'm back. Tell them, I know what they did, and I'm on my way. And if they ask you who I am, tell them I came the long way round.

His eyes… His eyes were the kindest, most terrifying thing I'd ever seen. As I ran for the citadel, I could still hear his words, as if carried on the wind or murmured directly into my thoughts. It felt as if everyone on Gallifrey could somehow hear him that day:

You can probably still hear me, so just between ourselves, you've got the prophecy wrong. The Hybrid is not half-Dalek. Nothing is half-Dalek. The Daleks would never allow that. The Hybrid destined to conquer Gallifrey and stand in its ruins is me.

He came to our home. I'd never realised, or never been told, that he'd once lived among us, back when he was no bigger than I was that day. He sat and ate soup, while we gathered around him, not one of us quite knowing what we could possibly say to him.

They sent a gunship for him, and he drew a line in the sand, then went back to his soup. They sent the General for him, with a platoon of soldiers, and he turned his back on them and walked

The Doctor's warm welcome

Gallifrey's army salutes its war hero

away. They sent all six of the Inner Council to abase themselves before him, and he slammed the door in their faces. Then, finally, Rassilon himself came for him. He was calling himself Rassilon the Redeemer by then, so convinced that Gallifrey owed everything to him, belonged to him. Rassilon the Redeemer stood in the desert, a General, a squad of troopers and a gunship at his back, and faced one unarmed man.

Get off my planet.

That was all he would say. Rassilon ordered his execution and, one by one,

the troopers dropped their weapons and stepped over that line in the sand to stand behind their war hero. Reinforcements arrived, more gunships, but they weren't there for Rassilon. Then the General spoke:

Lord President, with respect,
get off his planet.

That evening, we watched the wispy trail of smoke gently drift away through the clouds as a small shuttlecraft vanished among the Sky Trenches. Rassilon the Redeemer, Rassilon the Resurrected,

Rassilon the Deserted

The Doctor and Clara Oswald – the Hybrid?

Rassilon the Lord High President, Rassilon the Founding Father had at last left Gallifrey. The High Council were on the next shuttle.

For what it's worth, I don't believe the Doctor is the Hybrid. I think he was trying to put the Time Lords off the scent, or maybe just frighten them a little.

He was obviously right that the Hybrid was never going to be half-Dalek. There are plenty of other candidates, though. There is a girl, a splicing of Human and Mire, who will see the final moments of the universe, so the legends say. There was another girl, part-Human, part-wolf, who looked into the Time Vortex then emptied it into the Emperor of the Daleks and turned him to dust. Another, made half-Time Lord by a unique biological metacrisis, and yet another conceived in the Vortex and born half-Human, half-Time Lord. None of them quite fits, though.

But what if the Hybrid is not one person, but two? A dangerous combination of a passionate and powerful Time Lord and a young Human woman so very similar to him – companions who are willing to push each other to extremes?

The Doctor did not stay on Gallifrey after he banished Rassilon. He didn't become President and rule wisely and benevolently. Instead, he tried to unravel the Web of Time, risking everything to save the life of his friend, Clara Oswald.

And when he failed, he stole a faulty time-travel capsule, fled Gallifrey, and started careering around the cosmos, righting wrongs, defeating monsters and abducting Humans…

For Mandy – always
And for Lucy – my little star

ACKNOWLEDGEMENTS

I didn't expect to write another *Doctor Who* book after exploring
the Doctor's Lives and Times with James Goss for the fiftieth anniversary.
My thanks therefore go to:

Albert DePetrillo for commissioning this book anyway

Grace Paul for helping it on its way

Paul Simpson for hunting down errors

Lee Binding for being kind to it when it was struggling into life

Richard Shaun Williams for bringing a new dimension to some very old images

And especially to Richard Atkinson for his tireless and brilliant design work

23 November 2016